The Workhorse

by

Michael Walker

First Edition 2025

I0666756

The Workhorse© by Michael Walker 2025

First Edition 2025

eBook ISBN 979823275899

Paperback ISBN 9798218887902

"Juriel realizes that true wealth lies in gratitude, respect, and companionship—not in fortune nor the approval of others. He is left alone, changed by loss...

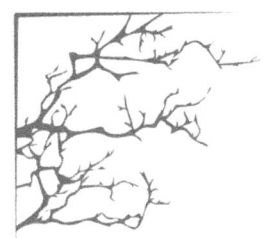

CHAPTER ONE

Juriel and the Onyx Horse

Dawn crept across the horizon like a shy visitor, brushing pale gold over the ragged edges of the scrubland. The world was waking inch by inch: first the distant rustle of sagebrush, then the flutter of a bird's wing, then the hush of morning wind dragging itself over the cracked earth. But none of this beauty mattered to Juriel.

Juriel had never been a man who greeted mornings with gratitude or awe. He woke each day with the same heavy sigh, the same determination to find riches that forever slipped through his fingers, the same bitterness wrapping around his heart like a stubborn vine.

He kicked at the ashes of last night's fire and muttered, "Another day, another disappointment unless luck finally decides to show itself." Beside him, tethered to a leaning post of dead wood, stood his horse — a creature so striking that even the sunrise seemed to pause for a moment, casting brighter light just to examine him.

Horse — for that was the only name Juriel had ever bothered to give him — was enormous. His coat was the deepest black imaginable, so dark it seemed to swallow shadows whole. When Horse moved, light traveled over him like water over polished stone. His mane cascaded down his neck like strands of midnight silk, and his eyes, dark and still, held a quiet intelligence that unsettled anyone who looked too long. He was the kind of creature stories should have been written about. But to Juriel, he was simply a beast to carry burdens.

Juriel stomped toward him, frustration already buzzing in his head. "You ate the oats again," he said, voice sharp as flint. "Those were worth coin, you stupid animal!" Horse's ears flicked back. He didn't step away or resist; he only watched Juriel quietly, that same unreadable depth in his gaze. The way he looked at Juriel was strange — almost knowing, almost patient. As if he understood something the prospector refused to see. That look only angered Juriel more.

"How many times must I teach you?!" The whip cracked through the air like lightning. Horse flinched, his muscles rippling beneath the onyx sheen of his coat. His hooves scraped dust. Yet he didn't fight back, didn't rear, didn't even snort. He simply endured.

A voice broke through the tension. "Why waste your strength on such a useless animal?" The whip froze midair. Juriel turned. An old man stood a few yards away, leaning on a crooked staff carved with swirling patterns. His clothes were simple, patched in places, the fabric the color of wood smoke and earth. His beard fell in soft waves to his chest, and his eyes — pale gray, sharp as winter frost — studied Juriel with a disconcerting mixture of pity and amusement.

The prospector scowled. "This is no business of yours." "Oh, but it is," the old man said lightly. "Everything is the business of those who still care to notice."

He pointed with his staff toward a narrow door wedged between two weather-beaten buildings Juriel swore hadn't been there yesterday. Above the door hung a dingy wooden sign so old the letters had worn away entirely. "Come here," the man said. "Inside. I've something to show you."

Juriel opened his mouth to refuse, but the old man's tone — calm yet oddly commanding — tugged at him. Something in Juriel's chest tightened in curiosity before he could stop it. He tossed the whip aside. "Fine. But make it quick. I have work to do."

As Juriel stepped toward the shop, Horse raised his head. For a moment, his dark eyes glimmered with something like alarm — or perhaps warning. But Juriel didn't notice. He was already ducking into the doorway, muttering, "Probably just another beggar with some tall tale." Inside, everything changed.

The moment Juriel crossed the threshold; the dusty world outside disappeared. The shop was vast — unimaginably vast — stretching upward into an arched ceiling so high it vanished into shadow. Suspended from that ceiling hung hundreds upon hundreds of crystalline ornaments: long spears of glass, bells shaped like frozen raindrops, spiraling rods etched with delicate patterns. They reached from above like the hanging gardens of some forgotten kingdom. Light filtered through cracks in the walls, catching the edges of the glass and scattering it in shimmering colors — sapphire, rose, emerald, gold. And then the breeze came.

A single cold breath of wind swept through the room. The crystals answered. They chimed — not randomly, not chaotically, but in a symphony so soft and haunting it felt alive. Each shard swung on its thin glass filament, all in different directions, yet somehow perfectly timed. The sound rose like the whisper of a thousand fairies singing from the heart of a mountain. Each crystal's note layered upon the next until the entire shop vibrated like a giant instrument.

Juriel staggered back. "What — what is this place?" "Ah," said the old man, strolling past him. "The music of things that are fragile but know how to endure."

Juriel stared upward, awe breaking through the crust of his hardened personality. "But how did you...? These things should break. They should fall." The old man chuckled. "Why would they fall? The floor is only a suggestion." Juriel blinked. "A...suggestion?" The man winked. "This is only your first visit. We must leave a few mysteries for later, mustn't we?" "...Be careful... I wouldn't want you to fall hm, hm, hmmm..."

The mysterious man lowered himself into a chair beside a small, cluttered table — though Juriel was certain that table had not been there seconds ago. "Sit," the old man said, gesturing. "Let me tell you something important."

2

Juriel hesitated. He wasn't used to taking orders, especially from wrinkled strangers in uncanny shops. But something in the air — maybe the soft singing of the crystals, maybe the old man's unfathomable calm — coaxed him forward. He sat.

The old man fixed him with a steady gaze. "You seem like a man always searching and never finding." Juriel bristled. "I find what I need." "Do you?" The old man said, as he raised a brow. "You carry hunger in your eyes. But not the useful kind. This is the hunger of someone who wants everything except what he already has."

Juriel crossed his arms. "If you're here to scold me, you can save your breath." "Scold?" The old man laughed — a thin, musical laugh that echoed strangely in the crystal shop. "No, no. I'm here to offer you something." Juriel leaned forward despite himself. "Go on."

"Adventure," the old man whispered, "and untold riches." Juriel's breath caught. Of all the words in the world, riches was the one that could penetrate even his stubborn heart. "Riches?" he repeated. "You mean gold?" "Gold," the old man echoed, his eyes gleaming like crystal facets, "and tests. You'll need both."

Juriel frowned. "Tests?" "You're a prospector," the old man said. "You've spent your life chasing treasure. But treasure without wisdom is simply a burden." Juriel waved a hand impatiently. "Enough riddles. If you know where treasure is, tell me where to find it." The old man's smile softened. "Ah. Straight to the point. Well then. It begins at the River of Treachery."

Juriel's face paled. Everyone in the region knew stories about that river — its violent currents, its unpredictable whirlpools, its strange habit of luring travelers into danger with mirage-like reflections on its surface.

"If," the old man continued, "you gather enough supplies — food, water, tools, and every needful thing — you may cross it. On the other side, you must restock." Juriel nodded slowly. "And then?"

"Then comes the ascent of Jagged Cliff Mountain. Higher than clouds. Sharper than nightmares." He traced the shape of the mountain in the air with the tip of his staff. "Few dare climb it. Fewer return." Juriel swallowed. "And beyond that?"

"Beyond," the old man whispered, "lies the Smoldering Pit Desert, a furnace of shifting sands and merciless heat." Juriel flinched at the memory of travelers who claimed their boots melted to the ground, of air so hot it shimmered like boiling water.

"But if you survive," the old man said, voice dropping to a hush, "you will find Tiny Mouth Cave. It sits exactly one hundred and one miles from the foot of Jagged Cliff Mountain — as the crow flies."

"What's in the cave?" Juriel asked, leaning so far forward his chair creaked. "Gold," the old man said simply. "More gold than you can imagine. Enough to make you the richest man in the realm."

Silence stretched between them. The crystal shop hummed. Juriel's heart thudded in his chest. "Why," Juriel finally asked, "would you tell me this? What do you want in return?"

The old man rose slowly, leaning on his staff. "I am on a long journey myself. One where earthly riches mean nothing to me. In exchange, I ask only this: that you be considerate of the things you have... and respectful to those who help you along your path."

"That's it?" Juriel questioned. "That's your price?" "That," the old man said softly, "is the most important part." He turned toward the door. Juriel blinked. "Wait — that's all you'll say?"

"If I told you everything," the old man said, pausing in the doorway, "you would learn nothing." He took one step into the morning light — then stopped. As Juriel stood up from the chair, preparing to rush out after him, the old man turned back and held something out in his hand: a tightly rolled parchment scroll, tied with a faded strip of red cloth.

"For the road ahead," he said. His voice was quiet, almost solemn now. "It will guide you where memory fails."

Juriel hesitated only a heartbeat before snatching the scroll. The parchment was rough under his fingers, heavier than it looked. When he glanced up again, the old man was already stepping out into the daylight. Juriel stuffed the scroll into his coat.

"This is it," he whispered, excitement burning through him like fire. "My chance!" He burst from the shop and sprinted to Horse, who lifted his head slowly, eyes reflecting the faint shimmer of the crystal shop behind them. Juriel swung onto his back. "Come, Horse! Adventure awaits!"

And with that, they galloped into the rising sun — never noticing that behind them, the crystal shop faded like breath on glass until nothing remained at all.

As the sun stretched into late afternoon, they approached a small frontier settlement hugging the banks of a shallow creek. A few cabins leaned against one another as though trying not to collapse. A water wheel creaked rhythmically, splashing water through a thin wooden channel. Children's laughter drifted from somewhere unseen.

The smell of cooking stew curled into the air. Juriel's stomach rumbled.

"We'll rest here," he said. "Maybe trade for supplies."

Horse slowed as they entered the settlement. Men and women working outside paused and looked up. Several stared openly. A few mothers called their children alongside.

Juriel frowned. "What's the matter with them?" Then he realized — they weren't staring at him. They were staring at Horse. Whispers rustled through the crowd. "Look at that creature..." "Never seen a coat so black..." "Eyes like ancient stone..." "He's too big to be from anywhere near here..."

Someone stepped forward. A young girl with tangled curls and wide hazel eyes. She approached Horse slowly, hand outstretched. Horse lowered his head and sniffed her fingers gently. The girl smiled. "He's beautiful." Juriel's first instinct was pride. His second was annoyance that someone else noticed what he preferred to ignore. "He's... fine," Juriel muttered. "More trouble than anything. You very well should be careful with your fingers, as I will not be held responsible, if any of them become missing... " The girl frowned. "He doesn't look like trouble to me!" Juriel huffed. "Shows what you know." Before the girl could reply, an older woman swooped in, pulling her back. "Don't bother the stranger," she chided, though her eyes stayed fixed on Horse. She lowered her voice, "There's something unusual about that animal..." Juriel bristled and grunted back, "He's just a horse." "Hmm," the woman murmured, unconvinced.

He tied Horse near a trough and stomped toward the trading post. Inside, the air smelled of sawdust, leather, and pipe smoke. A burly man behind the counter narrowed his eyes. "What do you want?"

"Food, water and supplies for a long journey," Juriel said. The man grunted. "Then you must have some coin to buy?" Juriel stiffened. "I... have a little..." Far too little, in truth. The trader snorted, "Then you can't afford much." Juriel slammed a small carving knife on the counter. "I can trade." The trader examined it. "There's rust, dull, not worth half a sack of barley!"

Juriel's jaw clenched, "Okay fine! Keep it!"

He stormed out with only two loaves of bread, a small bag of dried beans, and a half-filled waterskin. "That's hardly enough," he muttered. Horse watched him approach, eyes soft. Juriel loaded the supplies. "At least I've got this journey's start. The rest I'll get along the way." He did not notice the quiet worry in Horse's gaze — worry not of the journey's difficulty, but of Juriel's blindness.

As they prepared to leave the settlement, the little girl slipped forward again. "Sir?" she called. Juriel turned slowly. "Take care of him," she said softly. "He's rare." Juriel scoffed. "He's strong. That's all that matters." The girl shook her head. "Not rare like that. Rare like... important." Before Juriel could question her, the woman pulled her away again.

Horse watched them go. Juriel swung into the saddle with a grunt. "Strange town." They rode on and on, as twilight spilled across the land.

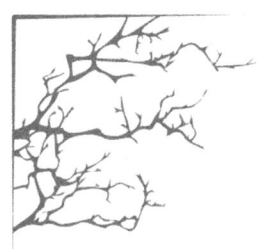

CHAPTER TWO

A Hasty Journey

The land opened in front of them like a great, empty book, every page blank except for the lines time had carved into the earth. As Juriel rode away from the old dusty town, he thought back to the crooked alley where the strange crystal shop had stood, but was no more. Now after tossing and turning through the night, Juriel barely waited for daylight to get back underway, as the morning stretched slowly over the horizon, bringing with it a steady warmth that softened the chill of dawn. Horse moved beneath him with patient strength, hooves thudding a calm, even rhythm against the dusty ground.

By the time the last buildings behind them shrank into distant shapes, the sun had climbed far enough to burn away most of the cool air left from night. A thin haze shimmered above the ground, rising from the packed earth and scattered stones. The breeze—light, warm, and tinged with the scent of dry grass—rolled across the plains in slow, wandering sweeps.

Juriel sat upright in the saddle, one hand on the reins, the other pressing occasionally against the inner pocket of his coat where the parchment map rested. He hadn't unrolled it again since leaving town, but the weight of it was enough to stir his thoughts again and again. He tapped the pocket with the backs of his fingers. "We've got ground to cover, Horse. The river's out there somewhere." Horse's ears flicked at the sound of his voice, but he kept his steady pace.

For the first hour, the land rose gently, rolling into low hills that seemed to ripple outward like frozen waves. Patches of sun-bleached grass clung to the slopes, bending and swaying with each passing breeze. Farther off, darker patches of brush gathered in clusters, sharp-angled against the softer lines of the hills.

Above it all stretched an enormous sky—blue at the top, pale near the horizon, with a scattering of stretched white clouds drifting lazily westward. One cloud in particular was shaped like a long, narrow feather, dissolving slowly at the edges. Another looked almost like a crooked spine, segmented and bent as if an enormous creature had left its bones behind in the heavens.

Juriel didn't bother trying to name the shapes. Clouds were clouds, and the sky was simply something overhead. His attention dipped instead to the earth beneath them and the faint line of darker land far ahead. "We'll stop up there," he said, pointing at a rounded hill with a rocky crown. "I want to see how far the land stretches." Horse didn't respond except to continue climbing.

As they ascended the slope, the crunch of gravel mixed with the softer thud of hooves on packed soil. The incline wasn't steep, but it was long, and the air warmed steadily as they rose. A single bird—a dark-winged, sharp-beaked creature—croaked from the branch of a stunted tree near the hill's crest. It watched them pass with one beady eye, hopping once along the branch before taking flight with a long eerie "caw... caw... caw..." disappearing in a rapid burst of beating wings. Juriel glanced at it briefly. Horse's ears twitched toward the rustling wings.

They reached the top of the hill and stopped. From this vantage point, the land unfurled in every direction, a wide sweep of gold, gray, and muted green. The hills rolled downward in slow, uneven folds, flattening into a long, broad plain where the grass grew sparser and the soil showed through like the worn hide of an old animal. To the west, the faintest glimmer of light flickered in a thin, wavering band—the suggestion of water far away. Juriel straightened. "That must be it. The river."

It was too distant to hear, but the shifting stripe of brightness was unmistakable. Even from here, the land dipped slightly toward that direction, forming a natural channel that any watercourse would follow. "We'll head that way until we find flatter ground. Then we can study the map." He gave Horse a small tug on the reins and began the descent.

The slope downward was scattered with stones that clicked lightly as they rolled under Horse's hooves. A few low shrubs rattled softly as they brushed past, releasing a faint, sharp smell — dry, resinous, almost smoky. Somewhere in the brush, a small hare darted away. Juriel caught only a glimpse: a flicker of brown, gray and white fur, a small tail, long ears pressed close to its head as it zig-zagged away.

By midday the sun was high and the air had grown thick with heat. The sky above had brightened into a nearly blinding blue, and the few remaining clouds drifted in thin, wispy streaks, offering no shade. Heat shimmered above the ground in wavering curtains, making distant shapes blur and ripple like reflections in disturbed water. Juriel finally pulled back on the reins. "We'll rest here a minute."

They stopped beside a narrow wash where the ground sloped inward, forming a shallow depression. Whatever water had once run through it was long gone, but at the very bottom, a tiny pocket of damp soil had collected a thin puddle—a few inches deep and no larger than a bowl. Horse saw it immediately.

Juriel dismounted stiffly and stretched his legs with a groan. "Don't know how far the river is from here. Might be hours still." Horse lowered his head and sniffed at the small puddle. The water was far from fresh—clouded with bits of soil and grass—but it was water, nonetheless. Horse dipped his muzzle into the puddle and drank. The soft sound of lapping water drifted up.

Juriel took the opportunity to pull the map from his coat. He unrolled it carefully, flattening it against his thigh as he crouched beneath the slanted shadow of a rock. His eyes scanned the inked lines again — the curve of the river, the angles of the hills, the long, unbroken plains that lay between here and the first major landmark.

The old man's script—thin but steady—traced distances and notes along the path. Juriel murmured the words under his breath. "West by a day... river crossing... then restock and go north toward the mountain."

He squinted at a tiny note beneath the river mark: "fast water, slippery stones"

"Hmph. I've crossed worse creeks than that." Horse lifted his head from the puddle just then, water dripping from his chin.

"You done? Good. That's enough." The prospector rolled the map again, bound it with the red strip of cloth, and tucked it securely back into the inner pocket of his coat. "Back to it!" he said, standing and brushing dirt off his hands. Horse shifted his weight as Juriel tightened the saddle and climbed back on. The puddle behind them rippled once in the breeze, then settled back into stillness.

The afternoon crawl across the plains was long and quiet. Little moved except for the occasional bird skimming across the sky or a distant herd animal ambling slowly along the horizon, too far away to identify clearly. The landscape itself seemed half-asleep, its colors softened by heat and distance. The sun leaned slightly westward, painting the plains with a golden sheen.

Juriel squinted at the sky. "Another few hours and we'll make camp."

The air shimmered around them, bending the lines of the earth into soft mirages. Sometimes the distant ground looked like a silver sheet of water, only to break apart into waving grass as they drew nearer.

Horse trudged on, sweat darkening patches of his black coat along the neck and shoulders, though he kept his rhythm steady. Occasionally his ears lifted at a faint rustle in the grass — a snake slithering out of sight, a ground bird hopping away with a flutter, an unseen creature darting through the brush.

A lone hawk circled above them, its wings stretched wide as it rode a warm current of air. It dipped once, twice, then rose again, scanning the land below for movement. Its sharp cry cut through the heavy afternoon heat. Horse's head rose slightly, watching the hawk.

As the day stretched on, the land slowly began to change—barely at first. The hills grew wider and flatter. The brush thinned. More scattered stones appeared—rounder ones, smoothed by long-ago waters that no longer flowed there.

At last, faint traces of greener growth appeared ahead, like a brushstroke of deeper color on the muted land. Juriel straightened. "A creek, maybe." Horse's pace quickened faintly, sensing water.

Thirty minutes later, they reached a narrow channel where a small ribbon of water trickled between stones. It wasn't much—little more than a long, shallow stream fed by distant hills—but it ran clear, and its surface rippled gently wherever the breeze skimmed across it. Juriel pulled back the reins. "We'll stop here a moment."

Horse stepped forward, lowering his head eagerly to drink from the stream. The sound of his drinking mixed with the quiet babble of the water over rock. Juriel crouched beside the creek, scooping a handful of water to splash against his face. The coolness startled him, and he breathed out sharply. He splashed again, then stood, wiping his brow.

"That's enough," he said after only a minute or two. Horse lifted his head, water dripping from his muzzle in small arcs that darkened the soil where they fell. Juriel tightened the saddle straps and mounted again. "Come on. We've got daylight left."

They traveled until the sun lowered into a warm orange disk touching the horizon. The sky shifted to soft purple near the east, streaked with pale gold clouds stretched thin as silk threads. A cool breeze emerged as the heat of the day began to fade. Juriel finally slowed Horse to a walk. "This is far enough."

The land around them had settled into a broad depression where tufts of grass grew a little thicker and the ground tilted gently, making a natural shelter from the wind. A low line of stones marked the edge of what might once have been a seasonal creek bed. Juriel dismounted and struck a foot against the dirt. "Hard ground. Good enough." He loosened the saddle but left it on Horse's back for the moment, then pulled a small bundle from the pack and set about gathering dry twigs and brittle stems for a fire.

A pair of small birds hopped nearby, pecking at seeds in the grass. One of them fluttered up to the top of a stone, tilted its head, and chirped out a quick, sharp song before darting away into the coming dusk. Horse lowered his head to nibble at the grass.

The fire crackled faintly once it caught, throwing a weak glow over the small clearing. Juriel sat beside it and ate a piece of dried bread and a few bites of tough cheese. He drank a careful swallow of water, then sealed the skin and placed it by his side. Horse lifted his head occasionally, chewing slowly, the muscles in his neck shifting under the fading light.

The sky continued to darken, stars emerging one by one until the whole dome above them glimmered. A faint breeze rustled the grass. Somewhere in the distance, a night bird called—a low, rhythmic hoot that echoed softly across the plains. Juriel lay back on a blanket and exhaled. "River tomorrow," he said softly to himself. "Then the real work begins." Horse shifted his weight, one hoof resting lightly as he dozed in a half-sleep.

The night settled around them in a calm, steady silence — the kind that belongs only to wide, open land and long, unbroken journeys. The fire faded to low coals. The stars wheeled overhead. And the plains stretched out on all sides, patient and unchanging, as Juriel and Horse slept at the edge of the next day's challenges.

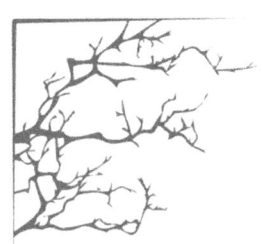

CHAPTER THREE

The River of Treachery — The Edge

Morning broke quietly across the plain, sliding in with a coolness that soothed the worn ground and softened the edges of the night. Pale blue light touched the horizon, spreading upward until the first slender rays of sunlight rose above the distant hills. The color of the sky shifted layer by layer — deep blue at the top, fading through soft gold, then warming into a steady, inviting brightness.

Juriel woke with a start, as he often did, as though sleep were an intruder he had reluctantly allowed into his camp for a few short hours. He rubbed his eyes with the back of one hand, stretched stiffly, and blinked at the scant plume of smoke rising from what remained of last night's fire. The ashes were gray and cool, and a faint charred smell clung to them.

Nearby, Horse stood motionless in the shallow hollow where the grass grew thickest. His dark form was still in the dim morning light, head lowered, one back hoof resting as he dozed lightly. A brief gust of wind rustled the grass along his legs. It also carried the faint sounds of waking land — the soft chirp of scattered birds, the distant rustle of dry brush, and the steady hum of the plains beginning their day.

Juriel pushed himself upright with a grunt and shook off the thin blanket he'd pulled over himself the night before. There were tasks to do. The day's traveling would not wait for sluggishness. He kicked a few stones aside and stretched his legs. The air was cool now, but it would warm quickly — that dry, biting heat that always rose from plains like these. He didn't bother with a fire this morning. There was no need. He would eat while the sun climbed and set out quickly to cover distance before midday. "Up we get," he muttered to himself, rolling his shoulders.

A few crumbs of dry bread and a bite of cheese served as breakfast. He ate standing, the morning breeze stirring the ends of his hair and the corners of his coat. When he was done, he brushed his hands against his trousers and took a slow, careful sip from the waterskin, mindful of every swallow. He glanced at Horse. "All right," he said. "Let's move."

Horse lifted his head at the sound of Juriel's voice, blinking once. Dew dampened the grass near his hooves, and a light trail of moisture lingered at the edge of his dark muzzle — the only drink he was afforded this morning.

Juriel cinched the saddle straps one notch tighter, checked the blanket to make sure it hadn't slipped in the night, and swung up into the saddle with a practiced motion. His boots settled on either side of

Horse's broad frame, and he gave a light tap of his heels. They moved out of the hollow and began a steady climb up the nearest rise.

The sky had brightened fully now. The sunlight grew warmer by the minute, casting long early shadows behind every stone and clump of brush. The landscape unfurled slowly as they ascended the slope. A faint sheen lay across the grass, sparkling where the dew still clung in the shaded patches.

Juriel took a deeper breath. The air smelled slightly of drying grass and the chalky scent of warm earth preparing for the day. He urged Horse onward with a small tug of the reins. "Come on. We don't want to lose the cool hours."

The slope leveled out at the top of the ridge, giving them a wide view of the plains stretching farther than sight could manage. The grasses moved in long, slow waves beneath the steady wind; patches of darker soil broke the continuity near distant ravines and old, dried streambeds. Juriel squinted into the west, searching. He saw them — faint at first, then clearer. The reflective glimmers of water, stretching in a long ribbon across the land. "That's it," he murmured. "Closer now." The River of Treachery. Still distant, but no longer a vague shimmer on the horizon. Now it was something solid, something approaching, something that would become the next test of the journey written on the map.

Juriel felt the map under his coat shift slightly as Horse moved. He put a hand over it as if to assure himself it was still there. "We'll check the crossing point once we're nearer," he said. "Can't judge it from this distance." Horse's ears flicked but his pace did not change. They began their long descent.

The land rolled downward in gradual, sweeping curves, the terrain packed with crushed, pale stones embedded in the earth. The rocks looked as though they had once belonged to a riverbed, smoothed by water long gone. Each step Horse took set a small crunch of gravel beneath his hooves, blending into the soft rustle of dry grass brushing against his legs.

As they traveled, a pair of small sky-colored birds darted through the air overhead, their wings catching the sunlight in brief flashes. They moved quickly, weaving in and out of patches of tall grass. They didn't come close; they didn't draw attention. They were simply part of the world, markers of the morning's calm. Juriel didn't give them more than a passing glance. There were many miles to cover. Birds came and went. The river was what mattered.

The wind changed direction as they descended. It grew warmer, carrying the scent of sun-baked soil. Juriel brushed a few strands of his hair back from his forehead. "It'll be a hot one," he muttered. Horse's stride remained firm.

They wound through a wide, shallow valley where the grass grew thinner and the earth showed through in long patches of cracked, pale clay. Dried weeds clung to the ground like brittle skeletons. To their left, a distant ridge rose in sharp, jagged angles before smoothing out toward the west. A lone boulder sat upright near the valley's lowest point, its surface carved by old winds into soft grooves and rippling shapes. Juriel guided Horse past it without slowing. "Keep going," he said quietly. The river drew nearer with every mile.

By late morning, the sound reached them. A low, steady rush — a constant murmur carried by the wind. It wasn't loud yet, just a presence in the background, like a grumbling conversation happening far away. The sort of sound that pressed faintly at the ears and told travelers that water was ahead.

Juriel straightened with a spark of energy. "There it is!" Horse's ears angled forward, but he didn't change pace. They moved toward the sound, over the crest of another rise, and finally the river came into full view. It stretched across the plains in a long, curving band, water flashing silver-white where sunlight struck its surface. The riverbanks varied — some gently sloped and lined with pebbles, others steeper with hardened clay. Clumps of coarse vegetation grew in scattered patches along the edges, bending with the breeze. Even from a distance, the water moved swiftly. The surface shimmered and broke in restless patterns, showing hints of depth and strength beneath the rippling light. And then there were whirlpools that would appear and disappear out of nowhere, sucking everything on the surface under and spitting them out hundreds of feet from where they were drawn under. Juriel exhaled slowly. "Well, then. We'll need a closer look." They descended toward the river.

As they neared the bank, Horse slowed a little, careful on the uneven ground where smooth stones lay scattered underfoot. Juriel leaned back slightly in the saddle to adjust his balance as they crossed the rough, descending slope. The air grew cooler here, touched by the river's mist. The scent of water drifted upward — clean, mineral, alive. At the base of the slope, the riverbank widened into a flat stretch of gravel and sand. The stones here were rounder, polished by endless years of rushing water. The sound of the river was stronger now, a constant rolling murmur that filled the air and drowned out the small noises of the plains.

Juriel dismounted. He walked toward the water until he stood at the very edge, small stones shifting beneath his boots with each step. He watched the river flow, analyzing its movement, its patterns. It was wide — much wider than he'd expected. The water twisted and curled in long rolling lines, its surface broken occasionally by small whirlpools or floating patches of foam. Bits of broken reed drifted sideways, swirling in the current. "Fast," Juriel muttered. "But not impossible."

He crouched and splashed a little water across his fingertips. It was cold — colder than any water he'd felt in recent days. A good sign. Cold water meant a strong current, but also a deeper, continuous source. He stood and looked upriver.

Somewhere along this stretch, the old man had marked a safer crossing point. Juriel reached into his coat, drew out the map, and unrolled it carefully. The parchment fluttered faintly in the river breeze. His eyes scanned the inked lines.

"There," he murmured. "Between two bends." He looked up, scanning the river ahead until he matched the drawing to reality. Two gentle bends created a curve that squeezed the river into a narrower passage. Rocks lined that bank more thickly. "That's it," he said, rolling the map again. "We'll move there." He tied the map securely and returned to Horse. "Come on."

They walked upriver along a narrow stretch of gravel. Horse stepped carefully over the stones, his dark coat gleaming under the rising sun. Every few minutes a breeze lifted the ends of Juriel's coat and stirred the grass beyond the riverbank. They reached the crossing point before midday.

The river narrowed noticeably here. Rounded stones jutted through the water, forming stepping points beneath the churning surface. The current still moved swiftly, but the banks were more even. Juriel looked across to the opposite side. "Not too far," he muttered. "We'll make it." He tugged the reins lightly. Horse followed him to the water's edge.

The river was loud here — not crashing or violent, but firm and insistent, as though reminding any traveler that the crossing would be on its own terms. Juriel looked up at the sky.

The sun was high now, burning white and bright. Small, streaked clouds drifted lazily, casting thin shadows across the plains. The temperature was climbing steadily. "Good enough," he said quietly.

He adjusted the straps on Horse's saddle, securing every tool, every bag, every scrap of supply. The terrain beyond the river stretched out in a long slope that gradually rose toward distant highlands — the path toward Jagged Cliff Mountain. Juriel tightened the last strap. "All right," he said. "Into the water." Horse stepped forward. Juriel mounted quickly and gathered the reins. The river hissed softly where the water rushed around stones. Horse moved into the shallows.

The cold water surged around his legs immediately, swirling with force. His muscles tensed beneath Juriel's legs as he braced against the current. "Straight ahead!" Juriel said. Horse obeyed.

The water rose halfway up his sides as he moved deeper. The sound of rushing water filled the air, drowning out everything else. Horse pushed forward, step by step, slipping once against a slick stone but regaining his footing with a strong surge. Halfway across, the current strengthened.

Juriel gripped the saddle horn. "Steady!" Horse leaned into the force of the river, muscles straining. Water splashed high along his sides. The current pulled hard, trying to drag them downstream, but Horse found footing on a hidden shelf of stones and pushed off again. The opposite bank neared.

One final surge. Hooves found gravel. Legs pushed upward. And Horse climbed out of the river, water streaming from his coat, the sound of the current fading behind them. Juriel exhaled and wiped a sleeve across his brow. "That's done," he said, though there was no pride in his voice, only practicality. He looked forward.

The land beyond the river rose in a long, slow incline. Beyond that incline, many miles ahead and half-concealed by distant haze, stood the first foothills leading toward Jagged Cliff Mountain. Juriel clicked his tongue. "Onward." Horse took the first step up the slope.

Behind them the river continued its endless movement, whispering over stone, rolling beneath the sun, indifferent to the ones who had crossed. Ahead lay long land, long miles, and the drawn line on a parchment map waiting to be followed. The journey continued.

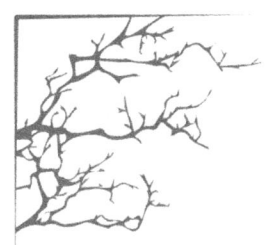

CHAPTER FOUR

The Far Side

The river's sound faded behind them as the slope rose, swallowed by distance and the low hiss of wind moving over the hills. The ground under Horse's hooves changed as they climbed—less loose gravel, more packed soil and flat stones embedded like old bones in the earth. Each step sounded solid and final.

Morning's brightness had deepened into a fuller light. The sun leaned behind Juriel's right shoulder as they took a gradual northward angle, warming his back and casting a long shadow ahead of Horse that stretched across the rising land.

The far bank of the River of Treachery gave way to a broad incline that seemed to lift them out of the plains and carry them slowly toward a higher country. The lines of the land grew stronger, the shapes of distant ridges clearer. The air felt drier here, and thinner, as if the wind had scraped it clean.

Juriel shifted in the saddle and rolled his shoulders once. "Good country for climbing," he muttered. "We make good time today."

Overhead, the sky stretched wide and cloudless at first, an open blue worth a painter's envy. As the hours passed, thin streaks of white began to form, high and wispy. They drifted in long chains, their edges feathered and dissolving into the blueness of the sky. A large bird crossed that open space, wings spread wide as it glided on invisible air currents. It passed without a sound, a small dark mark against the bright heavens until it tilted and drifted out of sight. Juriel barely moved except to adjust his grip on the reins. "Step up, Horse," he said quietly. "We've got a rise to the crest."

Horse's breathing grew heavier as the climb continued. Sweat darkened the fur along his shoulders and flanks. The huge muscles in his legs flexed and tightened beneath Juriel's weight with every stride. He didn't slow on his own. The slope demanded steady effort, and he gave it.

By mid-morning, the incline eased for a while. The ground flattened into a high shelf of land where the grass grew in small clumps, separated by dry gravel and cracked soil. A few low shrubs grew along a shallow dip, their branches twisted and tough, leaves narrow and silver-edged.

Juriel lifted a leg slightly to stretch a cramped thigh, then guided Horse toward the shrubs. The dip in the ground looked like the sort that might catch runoff during storms. Today, it held only dust. He stopped anyway. "Rest your legs," he told Horse.

Horse stood, sides moving with the rhythm of his breath. Foam had gathered in the corners of his mouth from the climb. He flicked his tail once, sending a few insects scattering away.

Juriel didn't dismount at first. He sat in the saddle, eyes scanning the land ahead. From this higher vantage, Jagged Cliff Mountain could be seen clearly for the first time.

It rose on the horizon like a jagged tooth biting into the sky. The lower slopes rolled broad and dark, but the upper ridges broke into sharp, uneven lines that caught the light in pale streaks of stone. Even from this distance, the peak looked torn, more like a row of broken blades than a single summit. Juriel narrowed his eyes. "So that's you," he said under his breath. "What a sight to see!"

He let his gaze travel along the approaches leading toward the mountain's base. The land between them and that distant bulk was a series of long ridges and shallow valleys, arranged almost like frozen waves. Farther on, the colors darkened, hinting at thicker stone and less forgiving ground.

He finally swung down from the saddle and dropped to the earth with a grunt. He untied the small bundle that held his food and tools, then walked a little ways off from Horse, scanning for any sign of water. There was none here. The air was dry and still.

He sat on a flat rock, unwrapped the bundle, and ate in silence. A piece of bread, a small strip of dried meat. He chewed slowly, jaw working methodically, eyes still on the distant mountain. Between bites, he took a single swallow from the waterskin, then closed it tightly. He did not pour any into his hand. He did not tilt the skin toward Horse. When he was done, he rewrapped his small meal bundle and stowed it away again. He stood, brushed crumbs from his hands, and returned to the horse. He checked the saddle straps, tightening one, testing the others.

"Enough standing," he said. "We're losing the cool of the day." He climbed back into the saddle and gave a light nudge with his heels. Horse moved on.

Behind them, the shelf of land sat quiet and empty once more, the twisted shrubs bending slightly in the wind that passed through.

As the day wore on, the slope became more irregular. Instead of one continuous rise, the terrain folded into layers of hills and cuts, some rising sharply, others sinking into narrow ravines. They followed the old animal paths where they could, but not all slopes were kind. Some were steep enough that Horse had to lean his weight forward and place his hooves carefully on scattered stones.

The sun climbed overhead, then drifted slowly toward the west. The light changed from a hard white to a deeper yellow, casting longer shadows from every rock and ridge. Those shadows stretched and pooled, gathering in the creases of the land like spilled ink.

From time to time, a small ridge animal moved among the rocks, sometimes visible for a moment before vanishing again. A set of long, slender legs flashed over a ridge line, then disappeared into a cleft. On another slope, a small shape paused near a rock and then slipped into the shadows. Juriel kept his eyes mostly ahead, looking for open ways through. The mountain drew a little closer every hour, its shape slowly enlarging in the distance.

The air grew warmer and drier by mid-afternoon. Juriel could feel the heat pressing against the back of his neck, creeping down under the collar of his coat. "Could use a breeze," he muttered. The wind eventually obliged, but not in any generous way. A hot gust swept up from the lower slopes, smelling of dust and sun-warmed stone. It tugged at Horse's mane and ruffled the ends of Juriel's coat.

They descended into a shallow valley ridge where the rocks lay scattered in greater number. As they passed between two larger boulders, a faint movement caught the edge of the scene — something small and quick slipping into a crack between stones. The sight came and went with no sound.

At the valley's center, they found a break in the ground: a seam cut where water once flowed long ago, now reduced to a narrow channel of stones. In a shaded hollow between two flat slabs, a shallow pool of collected water rested, barely deeper than a hand's width. Juriel pulled on the reins. "Stop." Horse halted. Juriel slid down from the saddle, boots crunching on loose stone, and walked to the pool. The water was still and clear enough to show the shape of the pebbles beneath. A small insect danced along the surface, leaving tiny ripples behind it.

The prospector crouched and cupped his hands into the pool, lifting water to his mouth. The liquid was cool from shade, and it ran down between his fingers as he drank, wetting his beard and jaw. He took a few small handfuls, swallowing each slowly, feeling the dryness recede from his throat. When he had taken his fill, he stepped aside.

Horse stepped forward and lowered his head to the pool. The small surface broke as he drank. The sound of his tongue drawing water was quiet and steady. Juriel gave him less time than the animal might have wanted. "That's enough," he said, turning away and tightening one of the straps on the pack. "We still have light. Move." By the time Horse lifted his head, Juriel was already back in the saddle.

They left the hollow behind, climbing out of the rocky cut and back onto higher ground. The small pool lay hidden again between its stones, reflecting a sliver of sky until shadow covered it.

The land ahead rose in a series of long, slanted ridges, each one higher than the last. Between them, the valleys narrowed. The earth grew rockier, and the grass sparser. Jagged Cliff Mountain now stood clear and imposing, its upper reaches pale and scarred where snow once clung in colder months. The lower slopes were darker, lined with broken stone and shadowed ledges. Juriel eyed it with a measured gaze. "We'll need to find a place to camp before we reach the foothills," he said quietly. "Not climbing that in failing light."

The sun had dipped lower, throwing the mountain's eastern face into deeper shade and tinting the western sky with early orange. Long ribbons of cloud stretched across the heavens, tinged with soft gold at their edges.

They crossed another rise and came upon a small plateau — a broad ledge of land where the ground leveled out before beginning its next ascent. A scattering of hardy grass and scrub dotted the area, and a few rocks offered partial shelter from the wind. Juriel drew Horse to a stop. "Here," he said. "We'll stop here tonight." He dismounted and rolled his shoulders, feeling the soreness settle into his back and legs. The day had been a long one, and the climb constant.

Juriel checked the packs, making small adjustments, tightening loose straps, shifting weight. He counted his supplies with his eyes, tracing each bundle and tool, his mind already measuring how far they would stretch: food, water, tools, the map pressed safely to his chest.

He took a modest evening meal—a handful of dried beans cooked soft in a small pot, a strip of meat, a piece of bread torn in half. He cooked over a low, controlled flame that danced behind a circle of stones. The smell of warm food hung close to the ground, carried only a little distance by the cooling air.

As the light faded, the sky shifted to deeper blue, then indigo, then black at the top. Stars appeared, one by one, puncturing the dark with points of white. Far to the east, translucent silver bands began to appear where the first hint of the moon nudged the horizon.

Horse stood nearby, reins loosely tied to a protruding rock. The animal's head lowered toward a thin patch of grass, but the pickings were poor, and the grazing short. Juriel ate, drank a measured swallow, and then sealed his waterskin. His movements were efficient, every gesture trimmed back to necessity. The fire burned lower.

Wind slid over the plateau, dragging along the shape of the land, making the grasses whisper in low strokes. The mountain loomed larger than ever in the near distance, its silhouette a dark tooth against the lighter sky behind it. Night settled in. And from somewhere beyond the edge of the plateau, in the dark folds of land still hidden from Juriel's eyes, eight shapes stirred among the rocks — it was wolves, eight powerful wolves paying particular attention to them.

They moved with practiced ease, paws silent on stone and soil alike. Their bodies blended with the lengthening shadows—gray and dark, mottled and lean. Muscles bunched and released under their fur as they climbed a low ridge and paused along its crest.

The wind carried the scents of the plateau: smoke from Juriel's small fire, the lingering smell of cooked food, the musk of a tired horse, the salt of sweat and leather and travel. The pack drew that information in through flared nostrils, testing it. Eight sets of glowing eyes adjusted to the dim light.

One of the wolves stood slightly ahead of the rest—a large one, its shoulders thick, its neck broad, the fur along its back raised just a little higher than the others'. It lifted its head, ears pricked forward, gaze fixed on the faint glow of the fire on the distant ledge. The alpha's jaw parted once in a slow, soundless breath. Behind it, the others watched as well. One wolf shifted its weight, tail flicking low. Another stretched its back in a fluid arch before settling again into a ready stance. They were not close enough to be seen from the plateau. The slope and curve of the ridge kept them hidden, their bodies outlined only against the darker stone behind them.

The alpha stepped forward, nose to the wind again, drawing in the camp's scent. The horse. The man. The fire. It began to move. The others followed, melting back from the ridge line and sliding down along a narrow path that hugged the shadows. Their movement was smooth and coordinated, spreading out along a loose arc that matched the shape of the land. They did not run; they loped, unhurried but intent. The plateau lay ahead. The man and the horse lay ahead. The wolves began to track them.

The day's journey ended for Juriel and Horse in hard-earned sleep, wrapped in thin blankets and the last warmth of the dying fire. For the wolves, the hunt had only just begun.

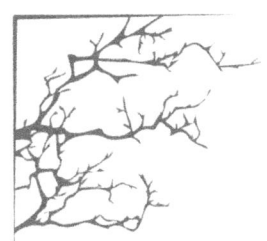

CHAPTER FIVE

Into the Foothills

The morning unfolded slowly across the plateau, first as a cool gray wash over the stony ground, then as a muted gold that reached across the slopes and drew back the shadows of night. Thin light clung to the edges of rocks and shrubs before spreading wider over the land. The fire from the previous night had collapsed into pale ash, its faint warmth barely touching the ground beneath it. A quiet breeze passed over the plateau, stirring the lighter leaves of the hardy shrubs and carrying the crisp scent of cold stone.

Juriel rose stiffly from his blanket, stretching his back and rolling his shoulders. The night had not offered deep rest, but he never expected comfort on such a journey. He folded the blanket neatly, secured it behind the saddle, and ate a quick breakfast: bread, dried meat, a measured swallow of water. He sealed the waterskin tightly. "Time to move," he said, more to the air than anything else.

He tightened Horse's straps with quick, practiced hands and mounted. The stallion stepped forward without hesitation. The plateau sloped downward into the rising foothills, a series of layered ridges leading toward the looming shape of Jagged Cliff Mountain. The land felt older here.

Stone broke through the soil in long, pale outcroppings. The scattered grass had turned more wiry, clutching to the ground in patches. The shrubs stood low and twisted, shaped by wind and sparse water. The morning air cooled slightly as they entered deeper folds of the land. Long streaks of cloud stretched across the sky, brightening as the sun climbed. The ridges ahead caught the light differently—first in soft gold, then in white as the sun crested higher, marking every curve and rise in sharp detail.

Juriel guided Horse along the slanted slope of the first ridge. Loose stones shifted under hooves, sliding down the incline in small clatters. The air was dry enough that dust rose easily, trailing behind them and drifting away on the breeze. The ridge leveled into a broad shelf. From this vantage, more hills presented themselves—some rising steeply, others rolling in softer curves. Between the ridges lay valleys cut with narrow dry channels and broken rock.

Horse carried Juriel across the first valley, the ground firmer here, packed by long seasons of wind pushing through the hills. A lizard warmed itself on a flat stone before darting into a crevice as the horse's shadow moved across the ridge. The climb became steeper as they approached the next rise. Horse leaned forward, pushing up the slope. Sweat traced dark lines along his coat. His breath grew heavier. Juriel allowed only a brief pause at a slanted rock shelf. "More to climb," he said, adjusting the reins. They ascended again.

The next ridge offered a broad view of the unfolding foothills. Jagged Cliff Mountain dominated the horizon, no longer a distant shape but a clear, massive wall of stone rising in jagged lines. Its flanks were dark where shadow clung to deep cuts and crevices, while the higher shoulders shone pale where the sun struck bare rock. Juriel stared at the mountain's face with measured calculation. "We reach the base tomorrow." He continued forward.

As the sun rose higher, the landscape grew harsher. The ridges tightened into narrow runs. The air warmed quickly, reflecting off stone and soil. Heat gathered beneath Juriel's coat and pressed against the back of his neck.

Elsewhere among the rocks, small ridge animals shifted in and out of shadow, their movements quick and soundless across the broken ground. The shrubs thinned as the ridges grew steeper, replaced by wind-smoothed stones and gravel. Juriel steered Horse along a twisting slope between two tall ridges. The narrow slanted cut offered temporary shade from the rising sun, though the wind there was thin and dry. At the far end of the passage, the terrain widened into a long terrace. A dry streambed wound across it, lined with smooth stones. In a small depression beneath a stone overhang, a shallow pool of water had gathered—a remnant from recent rainfall.

Juriel dismounted and drank from his cupped hands. The water was cool and clean, caught from shade and stone. Horse drank after him. Juriel gave him a short moment. Then he sternly said to Horse, "Enough, up." The journey resumed.

The land rose again in long, steady lines. Afternoon light traced the ridges in gold. Shadows gathered behind the rocks as the sun moved westward. The air thinned slightly as the elevation increased, carrying the faint metallic scent of older stone buried deep within the mountain's roots. They reached another ridge and followed its length to a broad, flat area near its top. Juriel halted Horse there. "This'll do."

He dismounted and prepared a small evening meal—just enough to quiet his hunger. A modest fire glowed between gathered stones. The warmth spread only a short distance before the cooling air took it. Horse stood nearby, finding a few sparse blades of grass to pull from between the rocks. The grazing ended quickly; the land offered little.

The sky darkened into a deep blue, stars appearing in scattered clusters. The horizon glowed faintly before fading as the last light slipped away. The wind carried the night's cold down from the higher slopes. Juriel sat with his back to a rock, coat pulled tight, eyes half-lidded from the long day. The fire dwindled, its crackles soft and infrequent. Night settled around them.

In the deeper folds of the foothills, far from the glow of Juriel's fire, the wolves moved. Their forms flowed through the shadows between rock and ridge. The land muffled their movement — their paws touched stone lightly, their bodies shifting in silent coordination. The alpha led them.

He was larger than the rest, broad-shouldered, thick through the neck. His fur stood in short, bristled spikes along his ridge. The moonlight caught the lines of his movement, showing the controlled, dangerous power in every step. The pack followed at a distance that matched his pace.

The scents of the man and horse reached them in thin threads carried by the wind—smoke, leather, sweat, the faint musk of the animal. The alpha stopped on a slanted piece of stone where he could draw the air more deeply. His nostrils flared. His chest expanded. His eyes narrowed toward the distant slopes where faint firelight touched the land.

Behind him, one wolf stepped too close. A younger one. Lean, narrow-shouldered, still learning distance and discipline. The alpha's head snapped sideways. No sound. No warning. He struck. The attack was sudden and fierce. Fangs flashed in the moonlight. The weaker wolf yelped once—sharp and brief—before the alpha drove him onto the stone, pinning him with brutal force. Dust scattered beneath their struggle. The weaker wolf kicked once, then stilled. The alpha held him a moment longer, teeth clamped near the throat—not biting through, only asserting the full weight of dominance—before releasing and stepping back. The younger wolf crawled away, tail low, body trembling. The rest of the pack watched without moving.

The alpha lifted his head toward the night air again, drawing the scent of the plateau. Then he began moving forward. The seven others followed immediately. Silent, coordinated, focused. The distance between the wolves and the sleeping camp grew shorter beneath the rising moon. Much shorter.

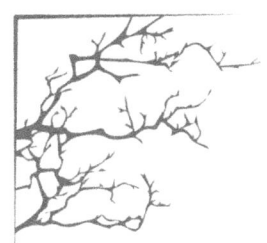

CHAPTER SIX

Something Follows

The morning came cold and still. The kind of cold that clung to the stones and made the breath rise in thin white streams from horse and man alike. Dawn arrived not with bright color, but with a steel-gray light that pressed gently across the foothills, removing the deepest shadows and revealing the shapes of the land one slope at a time.

Juriel stirred from his blanket, wincing as stiff muscles reminded him of the long climb from the day before. He sat up slowly, rubbing his arms to warm them, then rose with a practiced economy of motion. There was no hesitation in him — no lingering over comfort — only the habit of someone who understood that each day's work began the moment sleep ended. Horse stood nearby, head lowered, his long dark frame unmoving except for the faint rise and fall of breath. Dust from the foothills clung to his coat, softening its sheen but not its strength.

Juriel gathered the remnants of the fire, scattering the ash until the last traces of the camp blended with the stone around it. He ate a small meal, a bite of dry bread and a few pieces of cold beans saved from the night before, then took one swallow from the waterskin. He sealed it tightly. There was no water for Horse this morning.

The prospector tightened the saddle straps, fastened the coils of rope, checked the tools twice — hammer, chisel, small pick, the spare straps — all in their place. "We reach the base today," he said quietly as he mounted. Horse started forward at Juriel's cue.

The foothills rose steadily toward the mountain, each ridge slightly taller, each valley slightly narrower than the last. The land here was shaped by long seasons of weather — wind carving the stone, water marking faint trails along the slopes where runoff had once flowed. The hills layered upon one another like the crests of a vast stone ocean.

The morning light grew brighter, turning from gray to pale gold. As it did, Jagged Cliff Mountain revealed more of its rough face. What had appeared distant and enormous the day before now loomed impossibly large across nearly the entire horizon. The mountain's lower slopes swelled up from the surrounding land, ridged in places like the folded legs of some enormous creature resting beneath the earth. Farther up, the slopes twisted into sharper angles, pale streaks of stone cutting across darker areas where deep gullies scarred the surface.

Juriel steered Horse along a narrow ridge where the ground slanted and the stones beneath shifted in a scraping chorus. The air thinned slightly, growing dry and crisp. Wind swept through the higher cuts, bringing with it the cold scent of stone that had never been warmed by sunlight. The slope angled upward once more. Horse dug his hooves into the ground for traction. His breath grew heavier with the strain. "We're close," Juriel said, scanning the land. "Only a little more before the base."

The sky overhead stretched clear, a smooth uninterrupted blue except for a few bands of clouds lingering near the eastern horizon. These moved steadily, shaped by winds that did not reach this level.

On a distant ridge, a pair of mountain deer crossed from one shadow into another, barely visible against the stony terrain. But the pack had seen them, and in what seemed to be an instant the smaller deer was surrounded, then vanished into a blur of brown and gray and a cloud of mountain dust. And where there were once two deer, now there is only one escaping and bounding away, knowing not to stop and look back.

Shadows gradually shortened as the sun rose. By midday, the land flattened into a long, stony shelf stretching toward the final incline—the true foot of Jagged Cliff Mountain. The climb ahead was too steep, too direct to attempt without planning. As the map had warned, one wrong angle on the approach could lead to paths too narrow or unstable to traverse. Juriel halted Horse at the edge of the shelf. He dismounted, dust swirling under his boots as he landed. He reached inside his coat and pulled out the parchment map, unrolling it carefully. The red cloth tie hung loose from one hand as his eyes scanned the lines inked onto the parchment. The mountain path drawn there wound tightly up the western face. He looked up, turning slowly to match the drawn lines with the real ridges before him. A narrow upward cut — steep but manageable — ran along the shoulder of the mountain's lowest rise. "That's the one," he said. He rolled the map and tucked it away.

Horse stood still, nostrils flaring as he breathed in the colder air rolling down from the slope. Juriel took a step toward the incline and tapped Horse's side with the reins. "This way." They approached the first real rise.

The base of Jagged Cliff Mountain greeted them with a wall of stone. It was not smooth. It was not welcoming. It rose in abrupt, broken lines that climbed higher than sight could measure. The lower cliffs bore patterns of fractures where entire slabs had separated and sheared away long ago.

The path was not obvious to the untrained eye. Only by following the faint lines of worn rock leading up a diagonal cut could one see where feet had once stepped. Perhaps travelers had passed here long before Juriel's time — miners, shepherds, wanderers — leaving behind the knowledge of the mountain's approach. Juriel pulled Horse into the narrow shadow that began the climb.

The air cooled suddenly, as though they had stepped into a different season. The sun could not reach the path here except in brief slants of light where the cliffs broke open. The beginning was steep. Horse's hooves clacked against the large stones embedded into the path. Dust broke free and drifted downward.

The incline forced the stallion to lean heavily into each step. Juriel held the reins taut and kept his body angled forward to balance the weight. Higher they climbed.

The narrow path curved along the mountain's shoulder, a slanted walkway of stone that hugged the cliff. A fall here would send a man tumbling down the slope for a long, crushing descent. But the path, though narrow, was solid beneath Horse's weight. A small bird darted across the sky far above, disappearing behind an outcropping. Juriel's mind was on the climb. On the exact route the old man's map had marked. On conserving supplies. On the thought of reaching the desert on the other side. He urged Horse onward.

By late afternoon, the narrow climb widened again, flattening into a long shelf where the slope dipped back slightly before rising sharply once more. Here the land offered a brief rest, a place where even the wind slowed and collected in a quiet pocket. Juriel brought Horse to a halt.

The shelf overlooked the entire stretch of foothills they had crossed. From there, the land looked vast — a rolling sea of ridges and valleys, wide slopes cast in soft yellow light as the sun dipped lower. A quick glance back revealed the faint line of the River of Treachery shimmering as a monument to past conquests now just a distant memory.

The air held a crisp coolness, touched with the promise of colder hours ahead. Juriel took another measured sip of water and ate a bite of dried meat. He did not light a fire. They did not need one here. The stone still held some warmth from the day. Horse shifted his weight, then stood still.

Juriel adjusted a strap on the pack, checked the rope coils, and sat back on a slanted stone to rest his legs. For a time, he simply studied the next part of the climb. Tomorrow they would have to cross the steepest section, where the path turned sharply upward and followed the mountain's spine. That was where the true challenge began.

He planned quietly, eyes moving from ledge to ledge, tracing the possible route. Evening drew its deeper colors over the mountain. The wind lowered into a steady hush. The last bands of sunlight edged the upper ridges in pale fire before fading. Juriel exhaled slowly. "We camp here. The next stretch needs light."

He settled beside the stone wall that pressed behind them. Horse lowered his head and gave a faint, exhausted snort. Night arrived.

Far below them, at the outer edge of the foothills, the wolves advanced. The pack wound through the rocks with the quiet ease of creatures shaped for such terrain. Their paws touched stone lightly. Their bodies moved in shadows cast by stone ledges. Their ears tracked faint sounds carried through the hollows — faint traces of movement, fire remnants, and the scent of man and horse.

The alpha led, stepping onto a long slab of rock broken from the mountain during some ancient shift. His eyes reflected the rising moon before him. A younger wolf ventured too close to his flank. It was not a mistake tolerated twice.

The alpha turned sharply and lunged. Teeth flashed, sinking into the other wolf's shoulder. The force sent the smaller wolf sprawling against the stone. Dust lifted and settled. The rest of the pack watched without sound or movement. The alpha pressed down, jaws tight, until the younger wolf yelped once — a thin, broken sound — then lay still. The alpha released him.

The injured wolf dragged himself to the back of the group, trembling, blood darkening his fur. The alpha returned to the front, unhurried. He lifted his head, sniffed the air, and resumed forward movement. The others followed. Silent. Focused. Hunting. And above them, high on the darkening mountain shelf where Juriel and Horse lay asleep, the night carried no hint of the danger advancing from below. But the distance between them narrowed. Very steadily. Very fast.

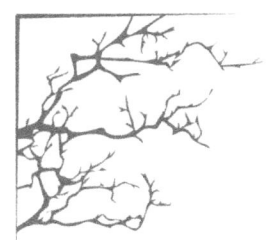

CHAPTER SEVEN

The Wolves Close In

The first light of dawn came late on the mountainside. The steep cliffs blocked the early sun, leaving the ledge where Juriel and Horse rested in a cool gray stillness. Frost clung to shaded stones. The wind had quieted during the night, but here and there it stirred again, pushing thin coils of mist across the shelf before thinning into nothing. Juriel rose from his blanket and flexed his fingers to warm them. The cold had seeped into his joints. He stretched once, braced his hands against the small of his back, and exhaled sharply as the ache eased.

Horse stood motionless near the stone wall, his sides rising and falling in slow, fatigued breaths. The strain of the climb—yesterday and the days before—lay in the heaviness of his limbs, the faint tremble in his shoulders. His dark coat was dusted with fine grit from the trail.

Juriel gathered what little remained of the night's warmth from the ground, scattered the dead embers of the fire, and ate his simple breakfast. Bread, a strip of meat, and one swallow of water. He strapped the blanket onto the pack, checked the tools and water again, adjusted the ropes, then pulled himself into the saddle with a quiet groan of effort. "The steep part's ahead," he said. "Let's get to it." Horse stepped forward onto the narrow trail.

The morning air sharpened as they climbed higher. The path turned from a gentle slope into a steep ascent that hugged the spine of Jagged Cliff Mountain. Here the stone changed color—from dusty gray to a smoother, darker surface with faint streaks of white running through it like veins. Wind skimmed across the ridge in steady gusts. It blew upward from the unseen depths below, carrying the scent of older, colder earth.

Juriel leaned forward in the saddle, gripping the reins and tightening his legs around Horse's sides as they approached the steeper bend in the trail. The path curled around a jutting outcrop of stone, narrow enough that Horse's hooves had only inches to spare. Below them, a deep hollow fell away for hundreds of feet. Above them, the cliff rose almost straight, marked by old cracks and ledges carved by seasons of storm.

The climb demanded Horse's full strength. His muscles strained, his breath deepened, and sweat traced new lines in his coat. Dust clung to his legs where hooves scraped against the rock. Juriel did not slow him.

The trail steepened again, turning sharply upward where the mountain grew more rugged. Loose gravel cascaded behind them with each step. The sound of settling stones echoed off the cliff walls. Wind pressed harder here, rushing along the exposed ridge. Ahead, the sun finally crested the mountain's upper shoulder, casting a pale, broken light across the narrow trail. The climb continued.

Far below, on the lower slopes, the wolves advanced. They had tracked Juriel and Horse through foothills, across ridges, around stone shelves, through gullies carved by forgotten rains. The trail had not cooled; the scent of sweat, leather, and lingering smoke clung to the rocks. The wolves did not hurry.

They moved together with the quiet expertise of seasoned hunters.

The alpha led with unwavering intent. His gait was smooth, powerful. His eyes remained half-lidded in focus, not from fatigue but from concentration. His breath plumed in steady bursts from his muzzle in the colder mountain air. Behind him, the remaining wolves followed in a tight, disciplined formation. The younger one who had been punished the night before limped slightly but kept his pace, driven by instinct and the fear of falling behind again.

The alpha stopped once to test the wind. The scent was stronger now. He turned his head uphill. The man and horse were close. He resumed the climb.

Juriel urged Horse onward across a slanted section of trail where the mountain's spine broadened just enough to allow safer footing. Here, narrow cracks broke the stone, filled with debris from landslides that had occurred long before his time. Small pebbles and loose dirt shifted beneath hooves, sliding downward and skittering into the vast hollow below. The air grew thinner. Juriel's breath shortened. Sweat cooled quickly on his skin. The wind tugged at his coat.

Horse climbed steadily, though the fatigue was clear in every strained breath he took.

The mountain revealed another plateau—not wide, but spacious enough for them to pause. Juriel guided Horse onto it. He dismounted but did not rest long. He ate a small portion of food, drank little, and checked the map again. The parchment fluttered in the wind, edges lifting. He traced the next line of the route. "One more climb," he said. Horse lowered his head but found no grass here. Only stone and scattered dust.

Juriel returned the map to his coat. "We push through." He mounted again and nudged Horse forward.

The wolves reached the previous night's resting ledge. They slowed near the scattered ash. The wolves circled the site once, testing the scents. The alpha lowered his head and inhaled deeply. His eyes narrowed. He stepped around the cold ash, looked up toward the higher ridge, and drew in a breath of the thin air. The scent was fresh. The man and horse had been here only a few hours before.

The alpha flicked his ears backward—a silent signal—and the other wolves fell in behind him. He began moving in a smooth, controlled trot, quicker now, driven by instinct and the certainty that the distance between predator and prey had shrunk to its smallest gap. A faint growl rumbled in his chest. The hunt tightened.

The higher climb demanded everything from Horse. The trail twisted sharply upward. Dust clouds rose with every step. The sun now angled across the ridge, heating portions of the trail while leaving other patches cold. The stone varied underfoot—some smooth, some rough, some fractured. Horse stumbled once. Juriel yanked the reins. "Up." Horse gathered his strength and pushed forward again.

The trail narrowed between two large stone shelves where the wind funneled through in a concentrated blast. It hummed between the rock faces, carrying thin grit that tapped lightly against Juriel's coat. The two weary climbers pressed on.

At last, the trail leveled into a narrow platform carved by nature into the mountain's shoulder. From here, the valley below looked like a great patchwork of ridges, slopes, and shadowed hollows stretching farther than any eye could comfortably take in. Juriel breathed harder than he would've liked to admit. Horse stood with his head lowered, exhausted. Juriel wiped his brow. "We rest here until sundown," he said. He dismounted and stepped onto the stone platform. Horse shifted his weight but remained standing. Juriel placed the pack near the stone wall and sat down.

The wind softened. Silence settled. Even the mountain appeared to pause. Then, a sound. Not loud, not sharp, but distinct. A scrape of stone. A soft displacement of gravel. Juriel turned.

Eight wolves stood at the edge of the platform. They emerged from the shadows in disciplined formation. Muscles taut. Eyes fixed. Breath steaming into the cooling air. The alpha stepped forward. Huge, broad-necked, teeth bared in a silent snarl. Fur bristling like a raised ridge of daggers. He locked onto Juriel.

Juriel rose quickly. He spread his arms wide, trying to make himself appear larger. He reached into the scabbard attached to his waist and drew his knife. "Go on! Get back!" he shouted. The alpha didn't blink.

Juriel stomped forward, pointing the knife at the alpha. "GO!" His voice hit the cliffs and fell into distant echoes. The alpha advanced. Slowly, deliberately. Head low, ears back. Eyes never leaving Juriel. Swinging the knife wildly, Juriel shouted, "Back!"

The giant black wolf opened his mouth wider. His breathing deepened into a silent, chilling growl. And then—The alpha lunged. He lunged straight at Juriel! Juriel barely had time to raise his arms before the wolf's full weight slammed into him, knocking the knife from Juriel's grip. The force drove Juriel backward against the stone wall, knocking the breath from his chest. The alpha's jaws snapped shut inches from his face, teeth flashing as they tore at empty air, trying to reach flesh.

Juriel slid sideways, scrambling to get away, boots slipping on the stone. The alpha pivoted instantly, paws scraping the rock as he turned his body to pursue. His muscles bunched, his shoulders lowered, and growling and baring his teeth — with fluid agility, the bloodthirsty wolf sprang forward to strike again.

In the same instance, Horse exploded into action!

The stallion reared, slamming his front hooves down between the wolf and Juriel. The alpha twisted aside, avoiding the full blow, but Horse did not hesitate. The massive animal surged forward with a fury drawn from exhaustion, fear, and instinct.

The wolf snarled and darted in, teeth grazing Horse's leg. Horse kicked. Hooves flashed. Stone cracked beneath the impact. The alpha dodged one strike but took the second along his ribs, the blow sending him skidding across the plateau's surface.

The wolf rose again—shaking dust from his fur—and lunged a third time, this time at Horse's throat. Horse spun sharply, hooves clattering against stone. With a powerful sweep of his hindquarters, he forced the wolf off balance. The alpha stumbled—just a fraction—but the misstep was enough. Horse drove forward and struck again. This time, the kick landed clean and full-force.

His hoof smashed across the alpha's jaw. The wolf's head snapped sideways with the force of the blow. Dust flew. The alpha collapsed onto the stone surface, rolling twice before coming to a halt. Silence hit the ledge with the weight of thunder.

The other wolves froze. Their eyes locked on the fallen alpha. He did not rise. His mouth hung half-open. His chest heaved once. Twice. A low whine left his throat. Then nothing.

The pack stood motionless. One wolf shifted backward. Another lowered its head. Without the alpha's certainty, the hunt unraveled. The wolves backed away slowly from the ledge, paws silent against the stone. One by one, they slipped down the trail, vanishing into the darkening path below.

When the last wolf disappeared from sight, silence filled the platform again. Wind brushed gently across the ridge. Horse stood trembling, sides heaving, sweat dripping from his neck.

Juriel stared down the trail where the wolves had retreated. He said nothing. He approached Horse, but only to check the reins and the gear. He searched around and retrieved his knife, placing it neatly in his scabbard. "You held your ground," he said quietly, though the words carried no warmth. He looked at the darkening sky. "We move at first light."

He sat down again, back against the mountain wall, breathing shallowly, holding his head in his hands in the cold air. The danger had passed. Night settled over the mountain. But the treacherous downward trek ahead remained.

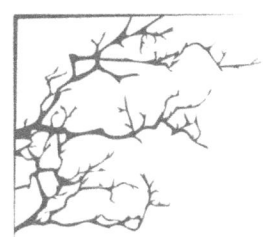

CHAPTER EIGHT

The Descent to the Cloud Ridge

Morning came thin and pale. Not the soft gray of the foothills nor the muted gold of the lower slopes, but a sharper, almost metallic light that pressed across the mountainside as though the sun itself had difficulty reaching this height. It seeped in slowly, filling the corners of the stone shelf where Juriel and Horse had rested after the confrontation with the wolves. The air carried no warmth. It sliced along the ridge in a cold whisper that danced across stone and tugged gently at Horse's mane.

Juriel rose stiffly from where he had slept. His blanket was cold to the touch, and thin crystals of frost clung to its edges. He shook them free with two firm snaps of his wrists and folded the blanket with practiced efficiency. He did not look toward the trail where the wolves had vanished. He did not linger on the events of the night before. He only moved with the deliberate, measured pace of someone who understood that the mountain itself remained the greater threat.

Horse stood in a shadowed crevice, head low. The stallion's legs trembled slightly with exhaustion, but he remained upright. Dust from the previous day clung to his coat in gray patches. Dried sweat made dark lines along his shoulders and flanks. Juriel approached him and checked the straps, tugging each one sharply. He fastened the tools again: the hammer, the pick, the tied bundles of rope. He tested the weight of the water and the small amount of food remaining.

The prospector ate his breakfast quickly — a handful of breadcrumbs and a small strip of dried beans — and drank a swallow of water. He sealed the skin.

"We descend today," Juriel said quietly, brushing frost from the saddle horn. "Make it through the downward cuts, and we'll reach the other side soon enough." He mounted, and Horse stepped forward, slowly at first, then more steadily as they approached the edge of the shelf.

The downward path began as a narrow cut in the stone, slanted and treacherous. Wind pressed through the crack like a living thing, weaving between the cliffs and carrying a low, sustained note that hummed in Juriel's ears — a sound not entirely wind and not entirely silence. The stone itself was darker here, polished smooth in places by ancient storms. Horse's hooves made dull, echoing thuds against the rock, and now and then a hoof scraped loose a small shower of gravel that bounced down the slope and disappeared into the vast hollow below.

Juriel rode hunched forward, balancing his weight over Horse's neck to compensate for the descent. His grip tightened on the reins as they moved downward in slow, careful steps. Above them, an unseen ledge broke the early sunlight into strips of gold and shadow across the stone. The pattern shifted as wind stirred through the cliffs. Flecks of light danced on Horse's coat, catching the dark fur in brief flashes.

The trail narrowed further, forcing them to angle sideways along the cliff. Here the world opened suddenly to their left—an immense expanse of ridges, valleys, and distant peaks, blurred slightly by thin mist drifting in the higher air. Clouds gathered far below, pooling in wide basins between the mountain ranges. They rolled against the lower slopes like a slow white tide. Juriel didn't pause. He urged Horse forward with a sharp pull. The descent continued.

As the morning wore on, the stone walls around them opened into a broader channel. The trail widened just enough for Juriel to lower his guard slightly, allowing Horse a moment to breathe without constant correction. Horse's breath fogged in the cold air. His muscles shook with fatigue, but he obeyed every command, moving carefully down the slanted trail.

They reached a flat shelf where the stone leveled. Here, faint marks etched into the ground hinted that others had passed through long ago. The gouges and shallow grooves looked as though once-taloned creatures or ancient tools had scraped across the ledge.

Juriel dismounted for a moment. His legs tingled from the long descent, and he stretched them quickly, shaking out the stiffness. He examined the route ahead, tracing the jagged line of the downward path with his eyes, noting where the stone split and where narrow channels would offer safer footing.

Horse stood still, his stance wide, steadying his weight after the long stretch of careful footing. His tail flicked once as cold wind pushed across the ledge.

Juriel took another swallow of water — small, measured — and secured the skin again. He moved to Horse's side, placed a hand briefly on the saddle, and then mounted again. "We move." The trail led onward.

The path soon narrowed into a set of switchbacks carved into the mountain's face. Sharp angles forced Horse to turn tightly, placing one hoof after another on narrow ledges. Dust and small stones fell away with each shift of weight.

The air grew warmer as they descended. Not warm in any comfortable sense, but less sharp, less biting than the wind of the upper cliffs. The mist drifting below thickened slightly, and portions of the valley ahead blurred into layered shapes of gray and pale green.

Juriel leaned back, bracing with his legs each time the path angled downward too steeply. His muscles strained with the effort, but he did not slow or soften his commands.

Horse continued forward without hesitation, though each step demanded precision.

Wind swept across the switchback cliffs, carrying faint echoes of distant stonefalls. The mountainside groaned occasionally — deep, resonant, the sound of shifting rock far below or far above.

They reached another flat stretch where the trail widened to the length of three horses standing side by side. Several natural pillars of rock rose from the ground here, tall and slender, each shaped by the elements into strange, layered forms. Thin cracks ran along the bases of some pillars, and faint traces of old water lines marked their surfaces. High above, sunlight filtered down through gaps in the cliffs, casting pale beams across the shelf. Juriel stopped Horse here. He dismounted. He removed a piece of bread, broke off a bite, chewed without hurry, and then lifted his eyes toward the next downward stretch.

The route ahead was longer, smoother, and more open than the switchbacks, but also more exposed to wind. A long slope of smooth rock curved downward, twisting slightly until it merged with the next outcropping. Juriel tightened the saddle straps again. Horse shifted beneath the weight, legs bracing. "We descend another ridge," Juriel said. He mounted, and they continued.

The slope was slow but steady, a long downward sweep that required careful footing. The stone was smoother here, its surface worn by countless storms. Horse's hooves clicked softly, the sound swallowed quickly by the vast openness around them. Mist rose from the lower slopes, sweeping in long thin sheets across the ridge. It wrapped around the stone pillars behind them and trailed along the cliff face in drifting wisps. The trail curved gradually, allowing glimpses of the valley below — wide, rolling expanses dotted with scattered rock fields and dark swaths of hardy vegetation. Farther still, the faint shimmer of water glinted in the distance, possibly the start of a river or a seasonal lake. As they continued the descent, the layers of cloud below grew denser, rising in slow billows that brushed the lower ridges like restless tides. Juriel kept Horse moving.

The slope leveled once again. They reached a narrow gap where the trail turned sharply between two towering slabs of stone. Here, the wind intensified. It poured through the gap in a concentrated rush, carrying dust and the scent of far-off rain. It tugged at Juriel's coat, pushed against Horse's flank, and rattled loose gravel across the ground. They pressed forward.

The path dropped into a long, slanted trough—one of the final downward cuts of Jagged Cliff Mountain. The rock here shifted from dark gray to lighter hues, streaked with pale minerals that glimmered faintly beneath the thinning sunlight.

Horse's breathing had grown deeper, heavier, each exhale fogging into the air before fading. His steps grew slower but remained steady, his muscles trembling briefly after each steep angle. Juriel urged him on.

The air warmed further still. The cold bite of the upper ridges faded behind them, replaced by a thicker atmosphere that hinted at the valley below. The trough opened into a broad landing carved naturally from the mountain's bulk. Part of the stone had broken away long ago, forming a flat area with scattered debris—chunks of fallen rock, slabs split by frost and time, and patches of coarse gravel.

Juriel halted Horse and dismounted. He walked to the edge of the landing. Before them shook the vision of the valley — a patchwork of heavy mist, rocky ridges, scattered trees, and distant water. The shifting white mass of cloud rolled against the lower slopes like a living creature stretching itself across the land.

Juriel wiped his brow. "We'll reach the valley floor today," he said. "Before sundown, if we keep pace." Horse stood still.

Juriel took a final sip of water, sealed the skin, and placed it back on the saddle. He mounted. They started down the final length of the trough.

The descent ended suddenly. The last slope dropped sharply, easing only near the valley edge. Here, the ground broadened, forming a gradual incline covered in coarse grass and low shrubs. The mist thinned as they moved downward, revealing clusters of hardy plants and patches of dark soil. The wind quieted.

The mountain loomed behind them—vast, towering, and now partially shrouded by drifting cloud. The land ahead stretched invitingly, though hardship still lay between them and the next step of the old man's directions. Juriel guided Horse to a small rise at the valley's edge and stopped. "We made it," he said quietly. Not with triumph. Not with relief. Simply acknowledgment.

The desert waited beyond the lower ridges—hot, merciless, and vast. But for now, they had crossed the mountain. Juriel slid from the saddle and stood still, breathing deeply as wind swept across the valley basin. Horse lowered his head, trembling faintly, but remained standing. Night would fall soon.

Juriel gathered a few pieces of dry brush, enough for a small fire, and stacked them near a natural stone wall. He ate. He drank a little. He rested with his back against the rock. The valley settled into silence. The mountain's shadow stretched long across the land. And in the cooling air, beneath drifting clouds and distant ridges, Juriel prepared himself for the harshest part of the journey yet—Smoldering Pit Desert.

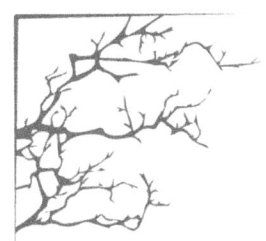

CHAPTER NINE

I nto the Valley Basin

The night settled over the valley in slow stages, as if reluctant to claim the land so recently touched by the last light of day. Shadows lengthened across the basin, gathering in the hollows between ridges and drifting along the uneven ground like silent tides. The air cooled, carrying the faint scent of mineral-rich soil and distant water, barely more than a whisper on the wind.

Juriel sat with his back against the natural stone wall, the remains of a small fire crackling quietly before him. The flames cast thin orange light across the ground, revealing scattered stones and the rough outline of the valley floor. He chewed slowly through the final portions of his meager meal and drank one measured swallow from the waterskin before sealing it tightly again.

Horse stood nearby in the dark, his shape outlined softly by the flicker of the fire. His sides rose and fell in deep, exhausted breaths. Dust clung to his coat, muting the dark sheen that had once reflected sunlight so sharply. The subtle tremor in his legs had slowed, but not entirely faded.

Beyond them, the mountainside loomed, half-shrouded by drifting cloud. The upper cliffs blended into the night sky, their jagged edges lost in shadow. The vast ridge they had descended now appeared almost unreal—more massive, more distant, more perilous in memory than it had seemed while they stood upon it.

Juriel allowed the fire to burn low before covering its remnants with a scatter of loose dirt. The gentle warmth faded gradually. He lay down beneath the stone wall where the wind could not scrape across him as sharply, pulled his blanket higher around his shoulders, and let his eyes close.

The valley remained quiet through the long hours. No wolves. No distant falls of stone. Only the wind sweeping occasionally across the wide basin in low sighs that stirred patches of grass and hissed against exposed rock.

The sun rose unseen behind the mountains, light reaching the valley only minutes later. It spread over the land in a pale wash, revealing the contours of ridges and the subtle sheen of thin morning dew clinging to the coarse grass. Juriel rose stiffly.

He folded his blanket, checked the water, re-tied the pack straps, and took a final look at the mountain they had conquered. "We move," he said as he mounted. Horse obeyed without hesitation.

The valley basin stretched wider than it had appeared from above. From the ridge, the landscape had looked like a single easy slope leading into gentler terrain, but from the ground it revealed layers—low rises, shallow dips in the earth, clusters of shrubby growth, and scattered patches of tall, dry grass that brushed against Horse's legs as they crossed.

The earth changed texture here. Instead of the gritty stone of the upper slopes, the soil grew thick and coarse, broken by patches of compact clay and sections of cracked earth. In places, thin lines of pale minerals traced patterns across the ground, the remnants of old runoff paths long since dried by sun and wind.

Horse stepped through the shifting terrain, hooves sinking slightly into soft earth before rising again. Mud cracked under his weight where dew had settled overnight. Dust swirled around his legs when he crossed drier sections. The morning warmed steadily.

Juriel rode in silence, adjusting the reins as needed while keeping watch on the uneven ground ahead. He marked the location of larger ridges, noted where deep shadows indicated steeper drops, and traced a mental route across the basin toward the far horizon where the land flattened. That border—barely visible in the soft haze—marked the beginning of Smoldering Pit Desert.

They crossed a shallow runnel where rainwater had once channelled through the valley. The ground here remained slightly damp, and small clusters of hardy reeds rose between cracks in the earth. Horse lowered his muzzle long enough to draw a few mouthfuls of this water before Juriel tapped the reins sharply.

Up they went again, crossing a series of ridges where dark stone broke through the soil, forming low walls of jagged rock. These ridges carried faint traces of heat trapped from days past, giving off a warmth that seeped into the air around them despite the early hour.

Juriel guided Horse over a break in the rock, choosing the path that offered the least resistance and the clearest angle toward the valley's far end. They traveled for hours.

By midday the air had warmed considerably. The valley's protective chill faded, replaced by a dry heat that clung to the skin. The sun emerged fully, its light bouncing harshly off pale soil and scattered stone fragments. Shadows shortened, shrinking beneath Horse's body in a small, dense patch that moved with each step.

Low hills began appearing more frequently as they continued forward. These hills rose gently from the earth, shaped by wind and time, their tops rounded and their slopes marked by faint patterns where water had once carved thin lines downward. Patches of dry shrubs clustered along the bases of these hills, their branches covered in thin layers of dust. Here and there, taller structures—long-dead remnants of desert trees—stood like twisted sentinels, their bark bleached almost white by sun and age.

Insects buzzed faintly in the warmer air, rising from grass patches in small bursts that scattered when disturbed. Their presence flickered briefly before fading again into the stillness.

Juriel slowed Horse briefly at the crest of one hill. From there, the true border of the valley revealed itself.

The land flattened sharply into a wide, empty expanse stretching toward an unreachable horizon. Heat shimmer rose from that distance even though midday was still young. A pale reddish tone colored the soil, hinting at the heat-trapped minerals beneath. Between the valley and the desert stretched a final band of terrain—a transition of pale, cracked earth that bore deep fissures and strange patterns carved by wind. Beyond that, the desert itself waited.

Juriel exhaled once. "We'll reach it by evening," he said. Horse lifted his head slightly but remained still. Juriel nudged him onward.

The final stretch through the valley basin felt longer than the distance suggested. The ground grew flatter but more treacherous. Deep crevices ran along the surface, forcing Juriel and Horse to weave between them. Some were narrow and shallow; others were wide enough to swallow a boot or break a leg.

Dust thickened in the warmer air. Horse's breathing deepened, though he maintained a steady pace. The shrubs grew sparser, then vanished entirely. The soil shifted from coarse grit to a smoother, powdery surface that clung to Horse's hooves and rose in thin clouds behind them.

Juriel adjusted the reins again, guiding Horse along a safe route between broken patches of ground. The sun pressed overhead, though still tolerable at this distance from the desert proper. The valley floor finally curved upward one last time into a gentle rise. Juriel urged Horse forward, and as they crested the slope — Smoldering Pit Desert unfurled before them.

It stretched in every direction but one. A vast sea of reddish soil, cracked like shattered pottery and marked by dark pits that dotted the land like ancient scars. Bands of darker sand streaked between these pits, forming swirling lines where hot wind carved across the open expanse. Heat shimmer rose already, blurring the horizon into a wavering line. The far edge of the desert seemed to dissolve into the sky, making it impossible to gauge distance or scale. Occasional ridges of blackened rock jutted upward like toppled blades. Some were tall and narrow; others lay half-buried in the sand, as though the desert had tried to swallow them but not yet succeeded. A few small plumes of rising heat twisted upward in wavering columns, the air above them bending in strange patterns. The land seemed alive with quiet, relentless warmth. Juriel surveyed the expanse in silence.

The old man's directions echoed in memory—cross Smoldering Pit Desert; bring every needful thing; do not underestimate its depth. Juriel slid from the saddle.

He stood at the edge of the rise for several moments, his breath steady, his eyes scanning the distant terrain. He loosened the pack straps, checked the tools again, and took a small drink of water. He did not offer the skin to Horse.

Horse stood motionless, ears shifting faintly in the dry breeze. Juriel mounted again. "We cross at dawn," he said quietly. He turned Horse back toward the valley interior, where a small natural depression offered shelter from the rising heat. They would need rest—even if only brief—before traversing such a place.

The sun lowered slowly behind the mountain they had left behind, sending a long shadow creeping across the valley floor. Juriel set camp without fire, using the valley's warmth instead. He ate sparingly and drank less than he desired. Horse stood nearby, unmoving except for the occasional shift of weight. The desert breathed its heat into the twilight. The valley darkened. And as night gathered over the land, Juriel closed his eyes beneath the muted sky, the old man's instructions lingering in the stillness. Smoldering Pit Desert awaited.

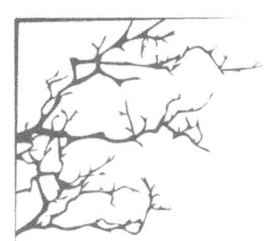

CHAPTER TEN

Smoldering Pit Desert

Dawn came thin and colorless. The first light did not spill gently into the valley as it had before; it crept over the rim of the world like a pale veil, stretching across the basin and laying itself over the land without warmth. The mountain behind them wore a faint, distant sheen along its highest edges, but most of its face remained in shadow.

Juriel rose, folded his blanket, and strapped it tightly behind the saddle. The air was cool for the moment, holding the last breath of night, but there was a stillness to it—a waiting—that promised a different kind of day ahead.

Horse stood near the shallow depression where they had taken shelter. Dust and dried sweat marked his coat in uneven patches, and the long climb and descent had left a tired heaviness in his stance. Yet his legs still held firm beneath him, and his eyes remained clear.

Juriel checked the straps on the packs, the loops of rope, the tools and hammer, the pick and chisel. He lifted the waterskin, weighing it in his hand. The amount left inside was not generous, but it would serve his needs for now. He took a bare swallow and closed it again.

There was no fire to scatter this morning, no ashes to hide. He had not wasted wood or time on flame the night before. Heat would not be lacking where they were going. "We start at first light," he said. He mounted. Horse stepped forward, and together they rode toward the low rise that separated the valley's last shelter from the beginning of Smoldering Pit Desert.

The climb to the rise was short but steep enough to draw a few heavier breaths from Horse. The soil here had already turned drier, the texture finer under hooves. Grass thinned along the slope, shrinking into shorter, colorless blades clinging close to the earth. At the crest, the world opened.

Smoldering Pit Desert lay ahead, spread out in a vast expanse of muted reds and deep browns, its surface broken by dark circles and irregular hollows that punctuated the land like open mouths. Heat shimmer had not yet risen in full, but even in the early light, a faint wavering disturbed the air above the distant ground. Long streaks of darker sand slashed across the desert in curved bands, tracing the direction of the prevailing winds. Black rock formations jutted up in strange, angular shapes, some jagged, some sloped and worn. They cast narrow shadows that lay thin and long in the morning light.

Beyond all of it, the horizon blurred—no trees, no hills, no rising mountain to mark a middle distance. Just sky pressing against land. Juriel did not linger at the crest. He tapped his heels against Horse's sides, and they began their descent into the first stretch of the desert.

At first, the change was subtle. The soil under Horse's hooves became softer, made of fine, powdery dust that rose with every step. It clung to his fetlocks and coated the lower half of his legs. Each hoof-fall produced a muffled thud instead of the crisp sound of contact with stone.

The air, still cool from the faded night, carried no scent of water—only the dry tang of mineral-rich earth and the faint bitterness of heated sand waiting for the sun's command. As the sun climbed, the desert responded.

The thin light deepened into something harder. The sky lost its early grayness and turned a bright, unbroken blue that seemed to stretch without end. The first sharp lines of shadow appeared behind scattered rocks, edges crisp and dark. The temperature began to climb.

Horse walked on, his breath steady for now. Juriel sat upright in the saddle, one hand resting lightly on the horn, the other holding the reins with relaxed control. There was no shade, no rise or hollow yet offering any shelter. They crossed the first wide stretch of level desert in silence.

The land slowly changed again. What had begun as a smooth plain of dust and fine soil gradually took on a different pattern. Darker circles appeared along the way—broad, shallow depressions where the color of the earth deepened to a brownish black. The soil in these circles had hardened and cracked, forming strange, irregular shapes that radiated outward like the remnants of dried pools.

The first of these pits lay off to the right, a large shallow basin with a floor fractured into jagged lines. The air above it trembled faintly, as if even this early in the day the heat gathered more eagerly there. Another pit appeared farther on, and then another, smaller but darker. They were scattered across the land at irregular intervals, sometimes grouped loosely together, sometimes standing alone. Between them the desert remained flat, broken only by the occasional rock or low ridge of baked earth.

Juriel kept Horse on a steady line between the pits. He did not weave needlessly among them. Only when a crack in the desert floor ran too deep or too wide did he angle Horse around it.

The sun rose higher. Heat gathered in layers. The desert began to live up to its name.

By midmorning, the air had turned heavy with warmth. The ground radiated heat from below, and the sun poured it down from above. A shimmering veil formed over the distant land, bending the horizon and making far-off shapes waver and blur.

Sweat trickled slowly along the back of Juriel's neck beneath his shirt. The inside of his boots grew hot. His hands, wrapped around the reins, felt the heated air pressing against his skin.

Horse's breathing deepened. Foam formed lightly at the corners of his mouth. Dark wetness grew along his chest and sides as his body worked to cool itself. His strides grew slightly slower, though his pace remained consistent.

A solitary, twisted desert shrub rose ahead, its thin branches leafless and gray. Its roots had found purchase in a crack in the earth where some small reserve of moisture must have once collected, though none remained now. Beyond it, a narrow strip of darker soil cut across the desert, its surface marked by faint lines where water had once run swiftly, carving shallow grooves that wind had since softened but not erased. Juriel drew Horse to a slower walk as they approached this old dry channel. At its deepest point, something different interrupted the monotony of cracked earth.

A shallow hollow lay at the channel's bend where an old pool had once gathered. A thin layer of water remained there, no more than a few inches deep, trapped in the stone basin. Its surface reflected the harsh sky in a dull, slightly muddied sheen. Horse stepped toward it without prompting, head lowering.

The water was warm from the sun's touch and faintly clouded, but it was water nonetheless. Horse drank, tongue pulling the shallow liquid into his mouth in slow, measured laps. Juriel let him drink for a short time—only as long as it took to empty the small basin. "Enough," he said at last. He gave the reins a firm tug and turned Horse back toward the open desert. The basin lay behind them, its last traces of water absorbed into the dry air.

As the hours accumulated, the day grew harsher. The sun stood almost directly overhead, turning shadows into small, dense shapes beneath rocks and pits. The sky glared down with relentless brightness. Heat waves shimmered across the desert in overlapping bands, making the far ground look like rippling glass.

The surface of the desert itself shifted in character once more. Dust gave way in places to harder-packed red earth, its surface scored by thin, intersecting cracks that formed intricate patterns. In other stretches, the ground turned almost black, as if scorched by some older, deeper heat. Near midday, they reached a stretch where the pits deepened.

These were not shallow, fractured basins but true hollows — great bowls carved into the desert floor, their edges steep and brittle. The soil inside them was nearly black, and from their depths rose a warmer draft of air that smelled faintly of old ash and stone baked far beyond the touch of ordinary sun. Juriel kept clear of the edges. Even Horse's hooves seemed to hesitate near the crumbling rims where the ground flaked easily away.

They passed pit after pit, some as wide as a small field, others smaller but deeper. The air above them flickered with heat, shimmering so strongly that it blurred the pits' true shapes. The land between the pits narrowed.

Instead of wide stretches of plain, there were now ridges of high, baked ground that wove like paths between these great hollows. In some places the space between one pit and another was no more than the length of Horse's body. Juriel guided him carefully along these narrow ridges. Sand and dust slid down the slopes beside them, whispering into the depths. By late afternoon, the desert had taken its full toll.

Horse's legs had grown heavier. Each step still fell in its place, but every motion had the weight of great effort. Foam dried in patches along his mouth. His sides rose and fell in slow, deeper draws of air. Juriel's throat felt dry and thick. He took another measured swallow from the waterskin, holding the liquid in his mouth before letting it slide down his throat. The sun dipped incrementally toward the west, but its intensity had not weakened yet. The sky remained clear. There were no clouds to offer shade.

The pits began to grow farther apart again, opening into a broader plain of hardened earth. Rocks appeared more often—low clusters of dark stone that had resisted the desert's shaping winds. In the distance, a narrow line of slightly raised land hinted at a ridge—nothing large, but enough to cast a small shadow when the sun finally lowered. Juriel set his eyes on that line. "We make it there," he said.

The desert stretched between them and that modest goal. The last of the pits, their edges crumbling and blackened, lay scattered along the way like warning marks. They crossed them at a steady pace. Dust clung to Horse's legs in thick layers. The air around them seemed to shimmer even at head level, creating a faint unease in depth and distance. The desert's surface appeared to shift slightly with each step, though the ground beneath hooves remained firm enough. As they neared the ridge, the first hint of a breeze slipped across the plain.

It carried heat with it, but also motion—a change from the still, pressing air that had held them for most of the day. The ridge finally rose before them, its height modest but sufficient to break the horizon and cast a narrow tongue of shadow along one side. Juriel steered Horse toward it. The shadow waiting there was small, but it was shadow. He stopped Horse in its edge and slid from the saddle, boots striking the ground with a dull, tired sound.

Juriel did not make a fire. There was no need. Even with the sun dipping toward the west, the earth held its warmth as though the day would never fully leave it. Juriel loosened the saddle straps slightly to ease the weight on Horse's back. He did not remove the saddlebags, only shifted them enough that the leather would not press in all the same places while the animal stood still. Horse lowered his head, drawing a few breaths that shuddered faintly with fatigue.

Juriel took a small portion of food from his pack—dried beans, a hard strip of meat, a bit of bread that crumbled slightly in his hands. He ate without haste, chewing slowly, giving his jaw time to work through the dryness in his mouth. He twisted open the waterskin. One swallow. He paused. Another, smaller swallow. He closed it again. The sound of the stopper turning into place clicked softly in the warm air. He placed the skin beside the saddle within easy reach for morning. Horse stood in the shadow, one hind leg relaxed as he shifted his weight.

The desert stretched out in every direction beyond the ridge, turning slowly from red to dull brown as the light faded. The sun slid lower, its glare easing. A softer, more golden tone settled over the pits and ridges. The heat eased a little but did not truly vanish. Far off, in the highest band of sky, a single bird crossed the horizon with slow, wide strokes of its wings, gliding on the rising air. Night gathered gradually rather than all at once.

The sky darkened from blue to violet, then deepened toward black. Stars began to present themselves one by one in distant points of white light. The desert cooled by degrees.

Juriel spread his blanket near the stone of the low ridge and lay down, boots still on, coat still wrapped around him. The ground beneath him radiated the last of the day's warmth. Smoldering Pit Desert lay quiet now—but not gentler. Only patient.

The old man's directions had promised that with enough food, water, and needful things, the journey could be made. Juriel had chosen how to measure "enough." The night waited over them. In the morning, the desert would test that measure.

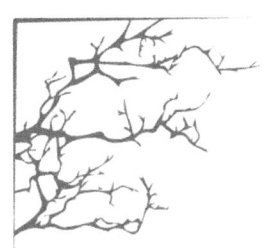

CHAPTER ELEVEN

The Laughing Maiden

Morning had not yet fully claimed the desert when Juriel awoke, but the land already radiated a dull warmth left over from the previous day. The ridge that had sheltered them through the night provided little relief now. The stone beneath him had cooled only slightly, and the air held the dry, faintly metallic taste of coming heat.

Juriel rose stiffly. His back ached, his muscles felt thick and heavy, and his mouth carried the sour dryness that water could not easily mend. He brushed the dust from his coat and checked the straps on Horse's saddle. The stallion stood motionless, one leg resting, head lowered, breath steady but shallow.

With practiced hands, Juriel tightened the packs, checked the tools, and lifted the waterskin. He weighed it again. There was less than yesterday.

He removed the cork and drank a single swallow. It sat in his throat like warm stone before sliding down, offering only the faintest moment of relief. He sealed the skin and hung it back on the saddle. "Time to move," he said.

He mounted slowly, settling himself against the saddle's heat-worn leather. Horse stepped forward at a steady, weary pace.

Dawn expanded across the desert in wide, unbroken light. The sky above shimmered as heat gathered from the ground below. No clouds drifted across it. No shade softened its brightness.

Smoldering Pit Desert stretched into the distance, a vast, undulating expanse of hardened earth and deep, cracked basins. Dark pits lay scattered like scars across the land, some shallow, some yawned wider, drawing lines of heat upward in wavering columns. Juriel kept Horse moving in a straight line. By midmorning, the heat intensified.

The sun pressed down like a weight. The air thickened. The shimmering distortions above the ground grew stronger, bending the horizon into a wavering band of red and gold.

Sweat slid down Juriel's temples but evaporated before reaching his jaw. His lips cracked, splitting with every breath. The skin on the back of his neck reddened beneath the relentless sunlight. His hands, gripping the reins, felt dry and stiff. His lungs strained with each inhale. Hot air filled him, offering no relief. Horse continued forward, his breath deepening, each exhale releasing a thin puff of steam-like haze that vanished instantly.

They passed a series of shallow basins where the ground grew darker, the heat rising from them in visible waves. Juriel felt it against his legs — thin, sharp heat that stung even through his trousers. The sun continued to climb. The desert pulsed. And the world slowly shifted.

Juriel's vision blurred at the edges first. Not with darkness or faintness, but with light — shimmering flecks that danced across the air like drifting dust. The desert's surface rippled, not from movement but from heat rising in layered sheets. Horse moved steadily. The horizon wavered. Juriel blinked once. Twice. The heat shimmer thickened, rising like smoke from the earth. The sky glared down in brilliant white. The pits on either side distorted, their edges curving in unnatural bends. Juriel forced his eyes forward. "Keep on," he whispered hoarsely. Horse obeyed.

Time stretched. The sun seemed to stand directly above them, unmoving. Juriel's head dipped once. He straightened. It dipped again. He jolted upright. His breath became shallow now, rasping between cracked lips. Sweat no longer formed along his brow. His tongue stuck to the roof of his mouth. His skin felt as if it had shrunk around him, pulled tight across bone and muscle. And then — a flicker of gold.

At first it seemed like the reflection of sunlight on distant stone—just a glint caught in the corner of vision. But it grew brighter. Closer. Shimmering like a small yellow flame twisting in the air. Juriel blinked hard. The shimmer began to take shape.

A figure rose from the golden haze – a luciferously-glowing figure, having the contours and mannerisms of a woman. She floated ahead of them, then beside them, then drifting just ahead of Horse's nose, but Horse did not notice her—as if the desert itself had breathed her into existence — out of heat and sand, placing her directly into the mind of Juriel. Her skin gleamed like polished gold. Her hair, long and loose, seemed to flow like molten metal. Her eyes glimmered with warm, liquid light. Gold makeup shimmered across her cheeks, her eyelids, her lips—so bright it almost reflected the desert around her. She smiled. And when she spoke, her voice was light, lilting, impossibly close—though she hovered where no shadow fell.

"Hey, you... stay with me." Juriel's breath hitched. His fingers tightened involuntarily on the reins. The maiden drifted a little closer, head tilting with a playful, teasing curiosity.

"C'mon... stay with me a while." Her laughter fluttered like the chime of glass ornaments in a distant wind. She circled Horse, moving weightlessly, her form shimmering at the edges as if lit from within by desert light.

"No?" Her smile widened mischievously. "No!!! Why not?" Her laughter spilled out again — sweet but brittle, like something bright hiding something sharp beneath.

"What's your hurry?" She leaned in, gold dust sparkling across her skin. "Hahaha..."

Juriel tried to lift a hand, to shield his eyes, to push her away, but his arm felt impossibly heavy. The maiden drifted backward, spinning gently in the heated air.

"**What did you come here for?**" she whispered, voice slipping into the space between thoughts. She floated beside his ear.

"**Hahaha...**" Then she moved to his front again, hovering above the shimmering desert heat. Her head cocked in sudden, exaggerated curiosity.

"**Did you bring enough?**" Her eyes widened like molten metal catching fire. "**Did you bring enough???**"

Her laughter burst out — bright, loud, echoing strangely in the heat and then dissolved into the shimmering air.

"**Hahahaha...**" Her golden form wavered, stretching and breaking apart like ribbons of sunlight and vanished.

Waking from a smoldering daze, Juriel sucked in air violently, as if he was breaking the surface of a freezing bottomless lake. It tore into him like cold air forced into burning lungs. He jerked upright in the saddle, his entire body shuddering then seizing. His fingers clawed at the reins, trembling uncontrollably. His breath came fast, sharp, ragged—each inhale scraping his throat like sandpaper. His heart hammered against his ribs. He stared ahead.

Nothing stood before them now. No golden shimmer. No drifting maiden. Only the desert —

endless, burning, wavering beneath the ruthless sun. Horse continued forward at the same steady pace, unbothered, the reins held taut in Juriel's shaking hands. Juriel dragged in another breath, forcing it past the tightness in his chest. The desert pulsed. The heat pressed. And the hallucination left behind only the taste of fear and the sound of fading laughter echoing through the dry, unforgiving air. The desert did not wait for him to recover.

Juriel now suffering badly from dehydration and exhaustion, sensed the need to move quicker, even though his body tugged at his mind, telling him to stop and rest. Instinctively he knew that if he stopped in the heat of the day in the middle of this blazing inferno, it would be the end of him, the end of all his dreams of riches and maybe even the end of his life.

He pondered as he rode, whether life without actually finding the treasure and having all his dreams fulfilled would even be a life worth living. But he would never know unless he pushed through and finished the journey. As the day wore on, he pushed Horse to the limit of exhaustion. Not out of spite, but out of sheer desperation, knowing that if they stopped short of shelter and a good place to rest, it would be the end of both of them. He could sense the angst in Horse's demeanor as his breathing quickened and his hooves hit the ground with a heaviness that could only come from a beast at the end of his limitations.

Looking to the west, as the sun began to move lower in the western sky, he could see strange rock formations colored in reddish layers with streaks of black running throughout them. Not too far in the distance but reachable, a little out of the way but probably necessary, because on the rock faces to the east and away from the setting sun, there was shadow. Blessed shadows, where they could have shelter from the merciless heat. So Juriel tugged on the reins, guiding Horse toward the rock formation. A little time passed and Juriel sensing Horse's struggle, he slid down off the saddle, landing onto the ground with a thud as a cloud of dust appeared underneath his feet. "This way," Juriel said, as he tugged Horse out of the ravaging rays of the sun and into what felt like a cooling waterfall sending streams of cooling air caressing every inch of his body. He immediately lie down, not thinking of having a meal, not thinking of drinking from the waterskin, only thinking of rest. He placed his head upon a cool, light-colored rock resting against the reddish clay rock structures that towered up into the sky. He closed his eyes and rested. Strangely, for the first time, Horse laid down and uncharacteristically displayed signs of giving in to the enormous workload that had been pressed upon him. Maybe for the first time, Horse was showing signs of weakness. They both rested and waited for the night.

Morning came, if it could be called that. There was no gentle coolness, no comforting softness to the air. The sky lightened, yes, and the darkness withdrew from the pits and ridges, but the heat seemed to have only stepped aside for a few hours and now returned with renewed intention. Juriel woke having the same sensation of dryness that he felt the night before he rested.

He pushed himself upright on stiff elbows, feeling the grit of sand under his hands. Dust had settled into the folds of his coat and blanket, into his hair, into the small cracks in his skin. When he flexed his fingers, tiny flakes drifted away from his knuckles. His lips stung when he closed them. Cracks had formed in the night — thin, red lines that pulsed with each movement. The skin along his nose and cheeks felt tight and sore, stretched from sun and wind.

Before Juriel awoke, Horse had already stood up and was now a few yards from where they originally rested. The shadow was gone now. The sun, only just risen, had already pushed it away. In this flat light, the stallion's coat looked dull, his muscles standing out in hard, clear shapes beneath the skin. When he shifted his weight from one leg to another, a faint tremor followed the motion.

Juriel stood and brushed dust from his coat. The waterskin felt lighter than he wanted it to when he lifted it. He opened the waterskin and took a swallow, rolling it across his tongue before he allowed himself to swallow. The warmth of the water made his stomach churn faintly, though he needed it badly enough that he took a second, smaller sip. He closed the skin.

He tightened the saddle straps, adjusted the tools and bundles, and mounted with more effort than the day before. His legs felt slower, heavier. His back complained as he settled into the saddle, as though the desert itself had reached into his muscles. "Forward," he murmured. Horse responded, stepping back out into the open desert.

The sun climbed quickly. What little coolness the night had offered vanished with startling speed. Heat slid over the desert in waves, rising from the ground and descending from the sky in a crushing, steady weight.

The pits scattered across Smoldering Pit Desert glowed darker now, their basins almost black beneath the burning light. The air above them twisted, the lines of the landscape warping in shimmering bends. Between the pits, the ground hardened, then fractured. Some sections were split into thin, curling plates that broke apart under Horse's hooves. Others held wide, yawning cracks that dropped into shadowed depths. Juriel guided Horse across the narrow ridges of intact ground. Dust puffed beneath each step.

Sometime during the late morning, sweat no longer formed on Juriel's skin. The dryness pushed too far for it. His lips bled in dots where earlier cracks had split further. His breath rasped slightly whenever he tried to take a deeper draw of air.

The blazing sunlight hurt. Not like a stab or a burn, but like a constant, unblinking stare that pressed on his eyes from every direction. He squinted against it, lines carving deeper into the corners of his face. The horizon wavered.

Far ahead, where the sky met the land, an indistinct darker smudge suggested a change in the desert — a ridge, perhaps, or a rise, or some broken line in the otherwise flat sweep. Juriel kept Horse pointed toward it without comment. They rode on fading into the distance and into the unknown and unpredictable fate ahead.

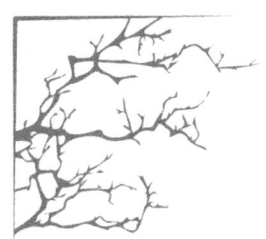

CHAPTER TWELVE

The Oasis and the Black Stone

The heat arrived long before the sun reached its height. It pressed across the desert in immense, sweltering waves, as though the air itself had thickened overnight into something heavier, something that clung to skin and bone and breath. Juriel felt it the moment he woke—felt it in the dryness coating his tongue, in the tightness of his lips, in the faint raw sting creeping across the bridge of his nose. His eyelids felt grainy when he blinked. His cheeks burned. The back of his neck pulsed with heat.

He sat up slowly, head aching from a night of restless, thin sleep. His hands shook slightly as he brushed sand from his coat. The rock formation that had sheltered them the night before had done little against the rising temperature; the stone beneath him radiated warmth as though it had never cooled.

Horse stood nearby, chest rising and falling in long, tired breaths. Dust clung to his coat in dull patches, and streaks of dried sweat created faint lines across his flanks. His legs trembled faintly as he shifted, though he remained steady.

Juriel reached for the waterskin. He lifted it. Even the slight weight felt too heavy. He drank only a swallow. The water inside was warm, tasting faintly of leather. It did nothing to quench the dryness that crawled along his throat, but it held back the dizziness clawing at his skull. He sealed the skin.

He tightened Horse's saddle straps, checked the tools, adjusted the packs with a grunt of effort, and mounted with more strain than he wished to admit. "Forward," he rasped. Horse stepped away from the ridge and back into the unrelenting openness of Smoldering Pit Desert.

The ground shimmered ahead of them. Each pit along the desert floor glowed darker under the rising sun, releasing thin columns of heat that rose and swayed in strange, wavering patterns. The air quivered above them, distorting the horizon until everything far ahead seemed to float.

Juriel's head throbbed. A deep, aching pulse behind his eyes made his vision blur at the edges.

The rising sun struck the back of his neck and arms, cutting through his coat as if it were made of thin paper. Sweat tried to form across his brow but evaporated before it could run down his skin. His lips cracked again when he tried to wet them with his tongue. "Just keep on..." he whispered hoarsely.

Horse obeyed, though each step landed more heavily than the last. Dust puffed around his hooves in soft clouds, which hung briefly in the air before vanishing into the desert heat.

The desert floor stretched ahead endlessly. The pits became fewer but larger. The ridges of hardened earth between them twisted in more dramatic angles.

Juriel felt himself swaying. His breath rasped. The heat pulsed against his skull. Time lost its shape. The desert became a rolling haze of red, gold, brown, and shimmering white as the sun climbed higher. It was near midday — though Juriel no longer trusted his sense of time—when the desert changed.

A faint patch of darker green interrupted the vast monotony. At first glance it seemed like another trick of the heat, but it did not shimmer away. It stayed. A small mound of color rising gently from the pale, cracked earth. Then a flicker of blue. Not sky-blue. Not mirage-blue. Water-blue! Juriel's breath caught in his throat. He blinked hard, trying to clear the blur clouding his eyes. The green patch grew clearer as they rode closer—literally growing from the ground, not wavering like illusions. Thick, wide-leaved succulents clustered in patches, their surfaces dotted with round, swollen fruits that bulged with moisture. Their leaves glistened faintly, catching light in a way no desert dust ever could.

A few taller stalks rose among them, bearing bulbous, pear-shaped pods with translucent skins stretched taut over liquid inside. And nestled among them — half-shielded by the greenery — a pool waited. A pool of water. Not filmy. Not muddy. Not shallow. A deep, sparkling well of crystal-clear liquid, fed by some unseen source beneath the earth. Its surface shone mirror-bright under the desert sun. Juriel felt suddenly weightless. Relief surged through him so sharply it made his skin prickle. The next moment, dizziness overtook him. The world tilted violently. The reins slipped from his fingers. His grip on the saddle horn failed. He fell from Horse's back.

He hit the ground hard on his side, dust exploding around him in a small cloud. He groaned, pushing his palms against the hot earth. His lips parted with a dry crack as he dragged in a gasp of burning air. He crawled. Every movement felt like dragging chains. The heat clung to him like a heavy blanket. His breath came in short, painful bursts. The pool shimmered only a few yards ahead. He clawed his way forward.

Sand stuck to his sweat-damp fingers. His arms trembled. His vision swam. He dragged himself until his knees struck damp earth — a texture so startlingly cool it shocked him fully awake. He lurched forward, nearly collapsing headfirst into the water. He cupped his hands and plunged them into the pool. Cold. Clear. Alive. He drank.

The first swallow sent a lance of pain through his throat. The second swallow felt like fire. The third, the fourth, the fifth finally quenched something deep inside him. He drank again and again until his stomach cramped with too much coolness too fast.

He plunged his entire face into the pool. Cold water flooded around his cheeks, his eyes, his nose. He held himself there until the burning behind his forehead eased. He sat back, gasping. There was fruit hanging abundantly from the succulent plants that stood like guards around the pool, fat leaves glistening with moisture. Fruits bulged, their skins taut and full. Juriel plucked one clumsily — an oval, deep green fruit — and bit into it. Sweet water burst across his tongue. His jaw trembled with relief as he chewed. He ate another. And another. Juice dripped down his chin, cooling the cracked skin.

He fell backward onto the damp earth, breathing heavily, staring at the crystal surface of the pool. For a long moment, he did not move.

Horse stepped forward, head lowering. Without instruction, the stallion reached the pool's edge and drank—long, deep, thirsty gulps. Water dribbled down his muzzle as he lifted his head between pulls, then he drank again. Dust slid away from his lips, falling into the pool before the rippling surface washed it aside. When he finished, he stood with his legs planted wide, as though the relief of water alone had not been enough to steady him fully. Juriel rose slowly.

His muscles felt strange — sore, but finally loose. His skin, though still burning, no longer felt like it was shrinking around him. He washed his face again, splashed water along the back of his neck, and let droplets fall down his arms. He filled the waterskin in full for the first time in days. He took another drink from the pool's edge before tapping down the cork. Then he saw it. The stone.

Half-buried in the sand, some yards beyond the pool, an oblong black boulder rose from the earth at a strange angle — leaning up and outward at exactly forty-five degrees, as though it had been placed purposefully, or had exploded from the ground mid-movement. Its surface was impossibly smooth. Not glossy — but polished in a way that looked unnatural. No cracks. No pits. No wind-carved grooves. Not even a clinging grain of sand. The stone's dark surface absorbed light without reflection, making it appear as though a piece of night sky had been carved out and set into the desert floor. Juriel stared at it for several long breaths. Then he reached into his coat pocket and pulled out the folded parchment map.

He unrolled it, the edges fluttering in the dry breeze. The faint ink lines traced the desert's emptiness with only a few small markings to guide the traveler. But one of those markings —

a small, dark oval drawn at a slight angle — sat in the very section of the desert they had now reached.

Juriel held the map beside the boulder and compared the curve of the drawn line, the tilt of the oval, the placement relative to the desert's pits. A slow, tired exhale escaped him.

The black boulder wasn't some accident of nature. It wasn't a curiosity or a stray shape in the desert. It was a **marker**. A deliberate sign. A guide. A fixed point the old man had known would lead him toward the strange cave tucked somewhere in this vast, unforgiving wilderness.

Juriel lowered the map and looked again at the boulder, its angled form pointing deeper into the desert—toward a horizon he had not yet reached. He touched the smooth stone surface with his fingertips. It remained cool. A silent, unyielding marker for those who dared cross Smoldering Pit Desert.

He folded the map carefully and returned it to his coat. Then he stepped back and turned toward Horse.

They rested until late afternoon, when the sun's fury softened into a warm but less deadly heat. Juriel ate more of the succulent fruit, filled the waterskin again, and stood for a long moment looking across the desert. The far horizon remained a wavering line, distorted by heat but clear enough to show one truth — there was still a very long way to go. He mounted Horse.

The stallion stepped forward, refreshed but weary. Juriel cast one last glance at the oasis. The shimmering water. The thick succulents. The impossible black stone pointing toward some distant part of the desert. Then he turned Horse toward the horizon.

The desert, though briefly forgiving, reclaimed its silence. As they rode, the oasis shrank behind them — a green patch swallowed by the endless gold-red sprawl. Juriel tightened his grip on the reins. The maiden did not return. No shimmering figures drifted across the heat. No voices called his name. Only the desert wind spoke — low, constant, whispering across the surface of Smoldering Pit Desert as man and horse continued deeper into its furnace.

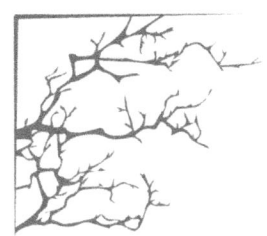

CHAPTER THIRTEEN

Harbinger of Destiny

The heat settled differently today. Not as a wave. Not as a blast. But as a weight — slow, heavy, unyielding—pressing down from the sky and rising from the ground until the air between felt thick enough to grasp.

Juriel woke to the sensation of it, lying on warm sand that had never cooled fully through the night. His blanket, though thin, clung to him with a faint, baked warmth, as if the desert itself held him in its grip. He pushed himself upright, joints stiff from sleep, and blinked into the morning light already gleaming across the dunes. His lips had dried again during the night; the cracks stung as he drew a breath and rubbed the dust from his eyes. The world glowed gold.

A sea of shimmering earth, shifting light, and the thin silhouettes of distant ridges.

Horse stood nearby, sides rising and falling in slow, tired breaths. His coat bore streaks of dried salt from old sweat, and dust coated his muzzle like powdered clay. He flicked an ear, gathering himself as Juriel approached.

Juriel checked the straps, the tools, the tightness of the ropes. He lifted the waterskin, felt its weight, and allowed himself one swallow. The skin's leather warmed instantly in the heat, though the liquid inside remained cool enough to refresh him. He hung it back on the saddle. "Onward," he said quietly. He mounted, settled into the saddle, and Horse moved forward into the blazing field of dunes.

The desert had changed. Not immediately, but subtly — the way the light fell across the ground, the way the pits lay farther apart, the way the sand formed deeper troughs between hardened ridges.

These troughs wound like ancient riverbeds—empty, carved long ago by water now replaced by heat. Thin ripples decorated the sand, shaped by winds that had since died away. Their soft patterns traced lines toward the far horizon, drawing the eye into the distance.

Juriel let Horse follow these natural grooves where the footing felt firmer. The rises along the sides shielded a portion of the wind, and the troughs funneled them toward the desert's center.

Above them, the sky shimmered. No clouds. No break in the blue. Only the sun staring down with relentless brightness. Time stretched in long, heavy minutes that folded into one another like layers of heat.

The desert offered no sound except the steady thump of hooves on hard sand and the whisper of wind brushing across scattered dunes. Each mile they passed felt deeper, drier, older—

as though Smoldering Pit Desert had shed all lesser trials and now revealed its truest form. Midmorning arrived before Juriel realized the sun had climbed.

Shimmering mirages rolled across the far distance—thin lines of silver that flickered and vanished, replaced by glowing distortions where the sky bent toward the sand. Some illusions rose like wavering towers; others curved like long rivers of reflected light. He ignored them this time.

Heat-waves rose so thickly that the land looked submerged beneath rippling water. The ridges beyond seemed to sway. The sky trembled at its edges. Yet Horse moved steadily, head lowered, hooves sinking slightly with each step.

Vultures circled far overhead, their dark silhouettes gliding across the sky on long wings before drifting away over the desert's outer ridges. A cluster of wiry shrubs appeared along a shallow dip in the ground, their roots twisted deep into hidden moisture lines beneath the sand. A few spiny blooms clung to them, pale and dry.

Horse stretched his neck toward the shrubs as they passed, taking a few mouthfuls of rough leaves. The stems snapped easily in his teeth, leaving behind thin, brittle fragments. As the sun pressed toward its peak, the desert floor began to rise.

At first the change was slight—a barely perceptible swell in the center of the land. Then the swell grew more pronounced, turning the troughs into long, slanting ascents. Sand slid beneath Horse's hooves as he climbed, leaving small avalanches behind them. Juriel's throat tightened from the dryness. His breath pulled through cracked lips. Sweat failed to gather along his skin; the air stole it too quickly.

When he guided Horse to the crest of one of the rising slopes, the land beyond stretched wider than anything they had passed yet. The pits lay lower now, as if they had settled into the desert floor, their dark hollows forming a crooked line off to the east. Between them, dunes rolled in uneven patterns, sculpted into long ridges by winds that had swept across them for ages. Juriel shaded his eyes with one stiff hand.

Far in the distance, beyond shimmering heat, a third dark shape rose faintly — a narrow, angled form barely visible through the distortions. Another marker. Smaller than the first one, or simply farther away. Angled just as the other had been. Black against the burning light. Juriel clicked his tongue softly. Horse continued down the slope toward the next long stretch of desert.

The sun reached its height. Heat fell down like a curtain. Juriel felt himself sinking into the saddle, shoulders heavy, arms numb. His skin burned beneath his coat. His lips bled in tiny red points whenever he forced them together. The back of his neck pulsed with a dull, consuming ache. Every breath scraped through his throat as though dragging sand with it.

Horse's breathing deepened; each exhale came with a faint rasp. His hooves left darker prints where their heat pressed moisture upward from deeper layers of sand.

The desert seemed endless. The horizon shimmered. The final slog approached from all directions at once. No cloud crossed the sky. No breeze eased the air. Only the slow progression toward the distant marker drove them onward.

Late afternoon softened the light, though not the heat. The sun dipped enough to cast longer shadows across the dunes, stretching them into thin, wavering lines that crawled along the sand. Juriel lifted the waterskin. One swallow. Then another. He sealed it quickly, forcing himself not to linger on its weight.

Horse stumbled once but recovered quickly, continuing forward without hesitation. His ears twitched now and then, responding to faint sounds of shifting sand or distant wind.

A few tall desert stalks rose from a shallow depression ahead, each crowned with pale yellow pods. Horse turned his head slightly toward them as they passed and tore away a few as he walked, chewing slowly with a faint, grateful snort. This was good, because Horse would need strength for the final stretch.

The desert narrowed again as they approached the faint black marker ahead. Sand rose in sweeping ridges on either side, framing a long corridor that funneled them toward the dark form. The sun dipped lower. The heat remained. And the second stone grew clearer. Near day's end, they reached it.

It rose from the sand like its predecessor — oblong, dark, angled upward as though pointing to some unseen place on the horizon beyond. Its surface gleamed faintly in the fading light, not reflecting the sun but absorbing it, turning the stone into a silhouette of pure, cold shadow against the golden desert. Juriel slid from the saddle.

His legs wavered beneath him, stiff and sore, but he steadied himself and approached the stone. Its surface was cool. Cooler than it should have been. Cooler than anything surrounded by desert heat. He touched it briefly, then stepped back and pulled the map from his coat.

A thin scratch, drawn in the same direction as the stone's tilt, marked this point on the parchment. Beyond it, only a short line remained. The last marker. The final stretch. The cave lay somewhere beyond this point — hidden in the desert's deepest span, waiting in the vast furnace of sand and heat. Juriel folded the map and looked toward the horizon where the stone pointed. The land stretched out in long, rippling waves of sand and hardened earth — harsh, unforgiving, a final test laid before him. He mounted Horse once more. "Onward," he said, his voice a raw whisper.

Horse stepped into the fading light. Their shadows stretched long behind them. The desert, vast and shimmering, opened to swallow them again as they began the last trek toward the far edge of Smoldering Pit Desert, where the cave waited in secrecy and silence.

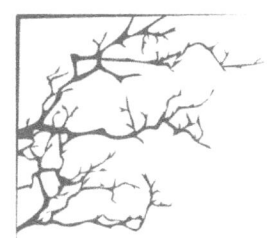

CHAPTER FOURTEEN

Everything and Nothing

The desert did not cool that night. Juriel had slept little, rolling on sand hot enough to seep into his bones. When dawn finally broke the temperature had risen rather than fallen. The sun glowed red at the horizon, its face blurred by heat that had never left the ground.

Horse lifted his head only slightly as Juriel stood. The stallion's breath came slow and steady, but drained. His legs trembled faintly beneath him, as if each moment demanded more from him than the last.

Juriel wiped dust from his coat, rubbed cracked skin at the corner of his mouth, and lifted the waterskin. It was still half full — heavy enough to carry hope, light enough to remind him that the desert had almost taken everything from him. One swallow. He corked it. "Forward," he rasped. Horse stepped into the rising heat.

The land changed as they neared the desert's heart. The dunes leveled into broad plains of pale, fractured stone. The pits lay behind them now, replaced by wide, shallow basins carved by winds so old they felt like ghostly memories. The horizon shimmered with violent waves of heat, enough to bend the distance like molten glass. But within that distortion — just barely visible through the rising glare — a dark shape appeared.

At first, it looked like another boulder. Then like a shadow. Then like the slanted outline of a cliff. And then Juriel saw it for what it was: An opening. Low, narrow, carved into the side of an outthrust ridge. The mouth of a cave, shadow-black and motionless in the boiling shimmer. Juriel's pulse quickened.

The cave. The one the old man had spoken of. The promise of gold left untouched by any other hand. "On..." he whispered. Horse responded, hooves dragging slightly in the hot dust.

The last stretch took hours. The desert fought every step. Heat rose in visible waves. Stone cracked beneath Horse's hooves. Thin dust lifted and swirled, stinging Juriel's cheeks like blown sandpaper. His lips split again, leaving a faint taste of iron on his tongue. But the cave grew closer. Its shape sharpened. The shadow within it deepened. The ridge around it curved like a natural gateway, leading them directly to its slender, dark mouth. At last, they reached the base of the ridge. The shadow cast by the cave felt impossibly cool even from yards away. It clung to the stone like a deep, ancient breath. It beckoned him inward. Juriel's heart hammered with excitement. He slid from Horse's back — boots scraping the stone, knees nearly buckling from thirst, but determination forcing him upright. He left the reins loose. Not once did he think of Horse's condition, nor pause to consider anything beyond the shadowed entrance ahead. Juriel stepped toward the entrance, eyes fixed on the darkness within.

The cave swallowed the outside world with a whisper of cool air. A welcome chill brushed across Juriel's face. His cracked lips twitched into something almost like a smile. The relief of shade washed over him, rinsing away the desert's glare. The entrance widened into a vast chamber. Juriel paused, breath caught in his chest. One step...Two...The air inside carried faint mineral scents—stone, dust, and something else. Something faintly metallic. Golden light glimmered from deeper within. It was not sunlight. Not reflected heat. It was gold—real gold—shining from the walls themselves. Juriel's fingers twitched. He moved forward, boots crunching softly on the sandy stone floor.

The first chamber stretched wider than any building he had ever seen. Natural pillars rose from floor to ceiling, ancient twists of stone formed by water long vanished. Some were smooth as polished marble; others had ridges like frozen vines. Golden veins laced through them—thin at first, then growing thicker as they twisted deeper into the rock. The walls glittered with streaks of yellow metal, glowing faintly in the shadowed light. Juriel approached one of the pillars.

The gold embedded within it was solid. Real. Untouched. He reached out, fingers brushing cool metal. His breath trembled.

He fumbled in his pack with shaking hands, gathering his tools. He pressed the tip of his pick to the vein. A single stroke. The sound cracked through the chamber like a bell. Golden fragments tumbled down. Juriel's heartbeat surged.

A laugh escaped him—sharp, breathless, triumphant. He struck again. And again. Each blow chipped more gold loose.

He filled the first canvas bag. Then the second. He piled handfuls beside his feet, greedy to take more, unable to stop noticing how quickly it came loose.

Riches. True riches. More gold than he had ever imagined. He paused only when his breath grew ragged.

Sweat beaded across his brow from exertion and excitement. His hands shook with adrenaline as he stepped farther into the chamber. The deeper he went, the richer the gold became. Thick veins. Great clusters. Sheets of metal shining like captured sunlight.

Some sections of the wall sparkled as if crushed gemstones had been pressed into the stone. Juriel ran his fingers across a thick golden sheet. His voice broke into the stillness. "All mine..." he whispered. The sound echoed faintly, as though the cave itself acknowledged him.

"All mine," he repeated, louder.

Years of hunger, years of empty pockets, years of dismissive glances from townsfolk who had called him foolish, desperate, hopeless — all of it seemed to crumble before the reality in front of him.

He imagined walking back into the village — bags of gold slung across Horse's sides, strangers' faces turning pale with shock, naysayers choking on their own disbelief. He pictured buying land. Horses. Livestock. A proper house. Fine meals. Silk coats. Everything he had ever been told he could never have. Fame. Comfort. Power. All of it within reach. He laughed again, breathless and wild. He plunged deeper still.

The cave wound downward into a long passage. The air cooled further. Moisture clung faintly to the stone. Small crystals lined the walls, glowing softly with reflected gold from deeper chambers. The sound of dripping water echoed softly somewhere below.

Juriel moved quickly, drawn by the promise of even greater treasure. His tools clanged against his hip. His eyes gleamed in the faint golden light.

The passage opened into a second chamber. Bigger than the first. Deeper. Rich beyond all reason. Gold spilled from the walls in thick seams. Massive chunks protruded like growths of glowing ore. Some pieces lay broken on the floor—natural fragments large enough to fill both hands. Juriel stumbled forward, overwhelmed. It was enough gold to fill pack animals for a hundred journeys. Enough to fill vaults in kingdoms far richer than his own. Enough to reshape his life entirely.

He ran his hands across the nearest seam — felt the cool, heavy metal beneath his fingertips —

and exhaled a trembling breath. This was what he had come for. This was what the old man had promised. This was the reward he believed he deserved. "All mine..." he whispered again, softly now. Nearly reverent. For a long while, he worked.

Tools clinked and rang. Gold clattered onto the stone. Small piles became larger piles. Juriel filled bags until they bulged, until the seams strained, until the weight grew punishing in his arms. He imagined all the gold he could carry back. He imagined future trips. Multiple trips.

Returning with wagons. With laborers. With entire caravans if needed. All under his command. His chest swelled with triumph. His breath came fast. Greedy. Hungry. He wiped sweat from his brow and looked deeper into the chamber, where still more gold glowed in the dim light. There was enough to return again and again. Enough to drown himself in riches. Enough to ensure he would never want for anything again. And he wanted more. So much more.

Juriel thought as he stepped deeper into the cavern, eyes fixed on the glittering veins ahead: behind him — outside the cave — Horse stood in the heat, loyally waiting for his return, reins hanging loose, strong and ready to carry the riches back to town. Juriel did not think of the heat or Horse's grueling load. Not once. Not even a flicker of thought. His mind was filled with gold. With glory. With the life he would finally have. With the endless possibilities stretched out before him like an open road paved in fortune. He tightened his grip on his tools. And the cave, rich with ancient gold and silent promise, swallowed him deeper into its shining depths — toward the final leg of his journey.

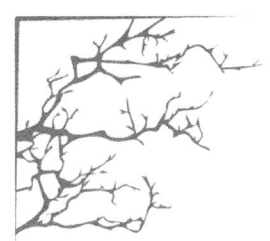

CHAPTER FIFTEEN

The Old Man's Lesson: The Needful Thing

Juriel worked until his arms felt weighted with stone. Time slipped out of rhythm inside the cavern. The coolness soothed his skin, numbed the sting of cracked lips and burned cheeks, and replaced the desert's oppressive heat with a sharp, beckoning thrill. The deeper chambers seemed to pulse with a strange, steady quiet — air shifting in the distance, drops of water falling from unseen cracks. Gold gleamed everywhere he looked.

He chipped it from the walls. He pried it from ancient seams. He scooped it from natural piles left behind by ages of shifting stone. Canvas sacks bulged at his feet—full, heavy, shining. The weight thrilled him. Gold was promise. Gold was future. Gold was triumph. He pulled out another bag and stuffed it full.

The cavern echoed with the sounds of his greed — clinks, cracks, panting breaths, the steady scrape of metal tools. He imagined the life ahead: rooms filled with wealth, food piled high, servants and fine clothing, a warm house with a hearth bright enough to chase away every cold memory of poverty he'd ever known. His hands shook with the thought of it. At last, he stepped back and surveyed his work.

Eight canvas sacks. Maybe nine — it hardly mattered. Each one stuffed with gold enough to buy a life better than he had ever dreamed.

He wiped sweat from his brow and slung one heavy bag over his shoulder. His muscles burned under the weight, but he lifted it anyway. The strain felt like victory.

He dragged the bag toward the tunnel that led to the entrance, its bottom scraping grooves through the sandy floor. The cavern air cooled his skin as he walked. He didn't hurry. Why hurry? He had won.

The entrance grew larger as he approached — a wide, glowing mouth of light and heat. Beyond it, the desert shimmered. The sun hung low, still fierce but drifting toward evening. Shadows stretched long across the ridge. Juriel stepped into the open.

The heat struck him like a hammer. He winced at the blast, blinking against the sudden glare. His skin, cooled by stone, felt instantly dry again. But he hardly cared. His eyes sought Horse.

The stallion lay collapsed near the cave mouth, legs folded awkwardly beneath him, neck stretched along the ground. Sand clung to his dark coat. His sides no longer rose and fell. His body was still. Juriel's brow furrowed, though not with grief — with confusion.

"Hah... come on now," he muttered, stepping closer. He dropped the sack with a heavy thud. "Up Up!" he said. The horse did not move. Juriel nudged him with the toe of his boot. Dust drifted from the stallion's body. No breath stirred from his muzzle. He knelt and pressed a hand against the horse's neck. Cold. Still. For a moment, Juriel simply stared.

The desert wind stirred a thin trail of dust across Horse's flank. The sun dipped lower, casting long shadows over the ridge. The air glowed gold in a way that felt almost mocking. His heart began to pound — slow at first, then faster. He looked toward the desert.

The line of dunes stretched endlessly. The ridges rose in shimmering waves. The horizon quivered beneath the heat. It was far. It was very far. His breath quickened.

He looked back into the cave — eight sacks of gold, shining in the dim light. He looked down at Horse — the body unmoving. The reins tangled loosely in the sand. The animal that had carried him through frost, wind, cliffs, wolves, and heat. The only creature who had borne every cruelty, every lash, every burden without complaint. Juriel swallowed, throat dry. The desert's heat wrapped around him like a closing hand.

"No..." he whispered. "No, no..." He stood quickly. He grabbed the bag at his feet and threw it over his shoulder again. The weight pulled him sideways. He stumbled but caught himself. He dragged it a few steps toward the desert. The sand shifted beneath him, swallowing each footstep. The cave mouth waited behind him. More gold. All the gold he could ever want.

He turned, breath heaving. Eight bags. He could carry them one by one. He could come back for more, make trips until nightfall, then again at dawn. He had time. He had strength. He had won. He told himself these things. But the desert didn't answer. It only glowed and shimmered and stretched out endlessly — a furnace waiting to claim whatever stepped into it. Juriel dropped the bag. It hit the sand with a muffled thud, sinking slightly. His chest tightened.

He went back to the horse and shook him again, harder this time. "Get up!" he snapped. "Do you hear me? Get up!" Horse never moved. Juriel's voice cracked. He staggered backward, eyes darting between the lifeless animal, the desert, and the wealth inside the cave. His breathing grew fast and shallow. Panic fluttered beneath his ribs. He stumbled into the cave mouth again, pacing in short bursts, running a filthy, sweat-streaked hand through his tangled hair.

"No... no... I can carry it. I can make it. I can—" He turned toward the desert again and took three steps forward. The heat slammed into him like a wall. His vision blurred. The horizon rippled. His throat tightened, and the first sliver of truth — sharp, unwelcome, undeniable — cut through the haze of gold-drunken triumph.

He needed Horse. He always had. He looked down at his own arms—thin, shaking, burned raw by days of brutal sun. He looked at the single bag he'd dropped in the sand. He couldn't carry eight bags. He couldn't carry five. He couldn't even carry one.

He lifted the bag again, straining. His knees buckled. He dropped it. He fell to his hands. His breath rasped. The desert's heat pressed down, heavy as stone. Behind him, the cavern glowed with its golden promise. Before him, the desert waited in silence, stretching out farther than any man could walk alone. Juriel lowered his head. "I... I can still..." he whispered, though the words shook.

The wind brushed faintly across the ridge — a soft, dry breath that stirred grains of sand across the horse's still form. Slowly, Juriel crawled toward the bag again, then past it, reaching the horse. He laid his hand on Horse's neck. The stillness felt like an answer. Juriel closed his eyes, breath trembling through cracked lips. Around him, the desert held its silence. The cave glowed behind him. The sun sank lower. He was alone. Alone with everything he had wanted — and nothing he truly needed.

He pressed his forehead to the horse's coat. As the heat deepened, as shadows stretched across the sand, Juriel realized the truth of his final needful thing — not gold, not tools, not water, not promises — but the companion he had lost through his own merciless ambition. The desert wind whispered across the ridge.

Juriel, surrounded by riches he could never carry and by silence he could not escape, let out a long, shaking sob. The journey had ended. But not at all as he had imagined. He then felt tired, very weak. Sleep grasp him by the temples and gold, thirst and pain and worry had slipped away. Time to sleep... Time to sleep...

THE END